The Ice Cream
Shooter Story

The Ice Cream Shooter Story

Written by:

Frank "Hot Shot" Rodgers

TIME: 12:26 pm & DATE: 2-12-2011

Better known as: "ICE CREAM" lead character in the story
<u>A Fiction Story and mostly created written story</u>

Introduction

YOUNG ICE CREAM'S DREAM

In the year 1971, young Ice Cream lived in an apartment with his family. Ice Cream loved the sport of basketball. He thought about basketball all the time. He consistently fantasized about being a professional basketball free throw shooter.

He started out shooting baskets at an early age, when he was just six years old. He made balls out of notebook paper with duct tape wrapped around them. He then took a brown grocery paper bag, cut the bottom out of it, and taped it on the wall in the living room in his parents apartment. Then he commenced shooting the homemade paper balls into the deluxe goal he had created. Ice Cream did not limit this activity to the paper goal; he also shot into small trash cans strategically placed throughout the apartment.

Chapter 1

FIRST GRADE

Ice Cream always focused on shooting paper balls. When he attended first grade at Bowling Park Elementary, he did not concentrate on his schoolwork. He sat in the back row, in the last seat to the far right of the classroom. Just eight feet slightly to the left behind him, Ice Cream noticed a small black metal trash can. *What a great time to practice my shots!* he thought. He took out his clean notebook paper, rolled it into paper balls, and made seven straight eight-foot shots during Mrs. Hoops's math class.

Mrs. Hoops's math class progressed. As she explained the math problems, she enthusiastically taught class and used the chalkboard as a visual aid. However, Ice Cream had other objectives; he continued to float paper balls through the air with precision into the twelve-inch trash can. Three of Ice Cream's classmates—Fats, Range, and Deep—watched him shoot. They liked the way he shot and decided to engage in the activity, but Ice Cream shot four times as much as the other boys.

"My turn, my turn. Watch this," Fats whispered.

However, as Mrs. Hoops taught class with her back toward the students, she heard the whispering; out of the corner of her eye, she noticed small circular objects floating through the air in the back of the classroom. She quickly realized the boys were the source of this odd event.

"Ice Cream, Fats, Range, Deep, stop throwing paper balls in the trash can!" she demanded.

However, Ice Cream continued to shoot the hand-rolled paper balls as he fantasized about being a professional free throw shooter. Mrs. Hoops decided to punish them, so she suddenly stopped teaching the class for a few minutes and hurried the boys outside the classroom to the hallway.

"But, but . . . Mrs. Hoops, I didn't—" Deep murmured.

"Stand here with your backs against the wall and do not move until I come back!" she interrupted with her hand in the "stop" position.

As she turned to go back to the classroom, Mrs. Hoops observed Deep as tears flowed down his cheeks. She returned to teaching her class undisturbed. Ten minutes later, she allowed the boys back in the classroom. As Mrs. Hoops ushered the boys back into the classroom, each student watched and giggled as the four shooters took their seats. Mrs. Hoops again continued to teach the class.

Twenty minutes passed. At this point, Good Pass, who sat two rows across from Ice Cream's desk, heard the crumpling of paper. She turned around to see where the rattling sound originated. Her three closest friends—Block, Dunk, and Set Shot—who encircled her by sitting on both sides and behind her, also noticed the familiar sound. The four dream boys were again the object of class disruption. The four girls just smiled. Good Pass liked the way Ice Cream shot; Block admired the way Fats floated the shots. Dunk grinned as Range shot, and Set Shot snickered as Deep made his baskets.

As the school year advanced, Mrs. Hoops realized the girls were close friends with the boys, but she did not know the source of the passion the boys possessed for shooting paper balls. Concerned about the boys' behavior, she asked the girls about the boys.

"I don't know," the four girls replied softly.

The boys continued to get in trouble, so Mrs. Hoops contacted their parents. Each boy stopped shooting paper balls except Ice Cream.

The second session of the school cycle remained. When the weather permitted, Mrs. Hoops took her class out to the playground. The four boys always headed to the basketball court to shoot free throws. The four girls always followed as they became interested in basketball. Mrs. Hoops, along with the other students, watched the boys and were amazed at their skill level. Mrs. Hoops then realized why the four dream boys loved to shoot paper balls into the trash can during class.

"Swish, one!"

"Swish, two!"

"Swish, three!"

"Swish, four!"

They made free throw shots without hesitation.

By the end of the school year, Mrs. Hoops appreciated the talent her young paper ball shooters possessed, but unfortunately, Ice Cream continued to be inattentive in class. Every report card Ice Cream took home to his parents reflected his inattentiveness, thus resulting in bad grades. Therefore, Ice Cream did not pass the second grade. His mother punished him, but his punishment did not end with his mother; his father also provided persuasive attention to Ice Cream.

Chapter 2

THE FAMILY RELOCATES

During the summer of 1972, Ice Cream and his family moved to another city. They settled in their new three-bedroom, one-bathroom, single-car-garage home. Not long after the move, Ice Cream's father purchased a basketball goal, and he mounted it on a twenty-five-foot pine tree in the backyard. This act of love made Ice Cream very happy. He practiced sun up until sundown the entire summer and many times until late at night. As darkness approached, he placed a drop light that he tied near the goal to enable the light beam to brighten the goal and the surrounding area. He spent most of his free time shooting baskets in his little heaven.

The end of the summer quickly drew near; therefore, it was time for the new school year to start. Ice Cream's parents registered him to repeat the first grade. This time around, Ice Cream was more serious about his class work; he did not want any more personal conversations with his father concerning his report card. He did not shoot his rolled paper balls into the metal trash can at his new school. Ice Cream remained focused during class sessions.

As with his old school, this new school observed a recess period. Again, some of the students followed Ice Cream to the basketball court to watch him deliver unyielding "swish." Everyone took notice of how well he shot free throws without ceasing. Thus, he had a successful social year with added friends, but more importantly, he demonstrated a successful academic year. So Ice Cream passed the second grade, and then the following year, he passed the third grade. His basketball skills continued to increase as he was promoted to the fourth grade.

When Ice Cream passed the fifth grade, his parents decided to allow him to play recreation community basketball; at this point, he was older and taller. He played for the Trailblazers on Saturday mornings. His family supported him by attending each game from December to February. As Ice Cream was the tallest player as well as the best free throw shooter, he played center. During one of his games with a tied score, a member of the other team fouled him with one second left on the clock. He went to the free throw line fifteen feet from the goal. Without hesitation, the basketball sailed through the air and straight into the nets. Cheers rang out. The second attempt again ended in all nets. The referee handed the basketball to the opposing team. The guard put a hurried shot up as the horn buzzed.

The crowd sang, "Air ball!"

As the chant echoed throughout the building, spectators leaped from their seats and rushed to the court to greet the Trailblazers. The excitement of the hard-earned win spread quickly throughout the gym like wildfire as members of the team jumped for joy.

"Ice Cream! Ice Cream!" they cheered as they clumsily placed him on the coach's shoulders.

Ice Cream's family never forgot the smile and laughter expressed by him at that very moment. As the season came to an end, the Trailblazers were recognized as they placed second overall in the district. With this recognition, each member received an eighteen-inch trophy. This was an inspirational season and one that Ice Cream never forgot.

Fats, Range, and Deep also played recreational community basketball where they lived. They each played important roles in their team wins. Successful free throw shots clinched the games for all the boys. Each boy talked with one another about their team wins and their free throw shooting percentage. During this time frame, the boys also called Dunk, Good Pass, Block, and Set Shot to talk about the successful season. The friendship that had developed in elementary school never lost its edge.

After the completion of the season, Ice Cream knew the fun of competition was over for a while. So it was back to the big pine tree, but as usual, on Saturdays, he had chores to complete.

"Ice Cream, go clean up your room and take the trash out," his mother stated.

"Yes, Mama," he replied.

As he quickly made his bed, he heard his father yelling down the hall, "Don't forget to wash the car!"

He wondered, *When am I going to get outside?* "Okay, sir," he replied.

Minutes passed. *Okay, I got the room cleaned. Now to wash the car. I hope I don't have to dry the dishes.* All these thought marched through Ice Cream's mind as his real desire was to put balls through the nets. *Oh man, I have to feed the dogs.*

"Finally, I'm done," he whispered. "Now I can practice my shots."

He picked up his worn basketball and went outside in the backyard to shoot free throws for thirty minutes.

Desiring to be around his friends, Ice Cream asked, "Mom, can I go to Good Pass's house so we can play basketball at the court down the street from the ice cream store?"

His mother answered, "Yes, we will take you, but first, you have to finish your schoolwork before Sunday. You know in the morning, you need to be ready to go to the early morning service."

"I did my homework, and I did it right," he responded.

His parents agreed and told him to be ready to come back home at seven forty-five.

"Good Pass, this is Ice Cream. I'll be at your house in a few so we can go to the court and shoot some free throws."

Fifteen minutes later, Ice Cream and his parents arrived at Good Pass's house. Ice Cream eagerly jumped out the back seat of the green LeSabre with his Wilson basketball at his side. As he exited, his mother reminded him of the pickup time.

"Yes, Mama," he uttered as he rushed to the side garage door, where he noticed Good Pass standing, waiting for him.

After a short discussion, they decided to ask Good Pass's parents if the rest of the crew could come to her house before going to the basketball court. Her parents were more than happy to have the kids assemble at the house. Therefore, Ice Cream called Range, Fats, and Deep about the plan to go shoot ball. However, just like Ice Cream, each young man had to verify with his parents if they could all meet up together. Their parents allowed them to go, but they each had a task to perform before leaving for Good Pass's house. Range had to iron his church clothes, Fats had to finish cleaning his room, and Deep had to let his father cut his hair.

After the boys received absolute confirmation from their parents, they called Block, Dunk, and Set Shot. When the three boys completed their small tasks, they were dropped off at Good Pass's house and reminded about the pickup times.

"This is great! We will all be together!" Ice Cream bellowed.

Chapter 3

THE CHALLENGE

Around 4:30 p.m., the youngsters left to go to the court to shoot free throws. Once arriving there, the girls took out their blankets and lay behind the basketball goal and eagerly watched their long-term comrades do what they did best. As the girls watched, they began to talk about the boys and became curious as to what was in their gym bags.

"Hide me," Good Pass whispered as she started to look in Ice Cream's bag. "I saw him talking to Vanessa. I wonder if she gave him a note or something."

Set Shot also became inquisitive and looked in Deep's bag. "I didn't see anything," she said with a sigh of relief.

As Set Shot zipped the bag back together, the girls noticed four boys and some girls walking up to the court. The young boys tossed the basketball around at the other end of the court, but it was obvious that they were watching Ice Cream and the crew. About fifteen minutes passed. The four boys approached the four dream boys and challenged them to a free throw contest. They accepted. All the eight boys agreed on the rules of the game. Each contestant would shoot for ten minutes, with two rebounders. Whichever team had the most baskets after four cycles would win the game. The girls would keep time for each of their friends. The tallest of the challengers, Big Raymond, pulled a dime out of his pocket and instructed Ice Cream to "call it."

"Heads!" Ice Cream shouted.

The coin twirled around in the air, tumbled to the ground, and landed on tails. Thus, Raymond started for his team. Ray put ninety-four shots through the nets, ending in an 80 percent success rate. His team members followed with positive results as well. Fats shot 102 free throws; 95 floated into the goal. As the contest continued, people swiftly started coming to the court and encircled the boys and took pictures and videos. The crowd cheered and watched with amazement.

"Oh man, that boy is bad!"

"I've seen him shoot before."

"Are you serious?"

These were just some of the comments screaming through the air.

The next shooter was Range. He approached the fifteen-foot free throw line and bounced the ball once, and then it was all nets. This shooting cycle continued until all the boys finished except for Ice Cream. Up to this point, the contest was tied. Ice Cream shot ninety-two successful free throw shots. The team needed two more blazing shots to win. Ice Cream tossed up a shot. It bounced off the backboard, twirled around the metal rim, and wisped to the left. Then Ice Cream observed the orange Wilson basketball drop to the worn cement. His heart dropped because he knew the clock ran out as he heard the time count down.

Ray approached Ice Cream with an intimidating smile. "I will see you later on down the road to beat you and your boys again."

Ice Cream didn't reply. He slowly walked away with his head hanging down in shame.

Chapter 4

AT THE ICE CREAM STORE

The team knew Ice Cream was deeply saddened by the events at the court, so they decided to treat him at the ice cream store, which was a block away from the park. They knew this would make Ice Cream feel better, for he loved to eat sugar cones with flavored ice cream.

After finishing his vanilla cone, Ice Cream noticed a plastic trash can. It reminded him of his old elementary school days. Once again, he formed a ball from his soiled ice cream wrapper paper and delivered it through the air to the trash can. It was just like they were back in the classroom with Mrs. Hoops.

"We'll be ready next time," Ice Cream proclaimed as wrapper after wrapper sailed into the distant trash can.

As they practiced their shots, the boys did not realize that a man who sat with his wife down the aisle watched them toss the paper.

While he and his wife were discussing their plans to return home, he told his wife, "Excuse me for a minute, honey." He rushed over to Ice Cream. "Can you shoot that shot again?"

Ice Cream answered, "Yes, sir, we can shoot it again."

The gentleman remarked, "Let me see it again."

Fats went back to the trash can and retrieved the paper wrappers. One at a time, each of the four dream boys made his shot into the lone standing trash can.

"That's excellent," proclaimed the curious man. He immediately asked the boys if they could make ten shots in a row.

The boys smiled and laughed as Range declared, "Without a doubt, sir."

This time, Ice Cream took the balls out of the topless trash can. Fats went first. All ten shots went into the trash can quite easily. Range and Deep followed with continued success. Ice Cream completed the paper ball toss.

"Forty attempts. Forty shots made," Deep affirmed.

"And at fifteen feet!" Ice Cream declared.

At this point, the couple was amazed at what the boys had just accomplished.

The gentleman proceeded to introduce himself. "My name is Coach Blue, and this my wife, Mrs. Blue. We are from Los Angeles."

Ice Cream then introduced himself, Fats, Range, and Deep. Then each young man introduced the girls. Ice Cream introduced Good Pass, Fats introduced Block, Range presented Dunk, and Deep introduced Set Shot.

Coach Blue replied, "It is nice to meet you young people."

"Nice to meet you also, sir," voiced the crew.

"Where are you guys from? And how long have you been shooting like that?" asked the coach.

"Since the first grade," Range replied.

"Really?" questioned Coach Blue.

"Yes, sir!" they asserted.

At that point, the coach expressed interest in seeing the young fellows shoot on the court before he left to go back to LA.

The boys knew they had to attend church on Sunday morning, so Range stated, "If it's okay with our folks, we can meet at 4:00 p.m."

Therefore, contingent arrangements were made to meet Coach Blue the following day at the basketball court, which was a block away.

As the coach handed Ice Cream a business card, he stated, "This is my hotel and room number on the back of my card to give to your parents if they want to talk with us. I am the head basketball coach at USC in Los Angeles. You guys will be going to high school to play on the basketball team, right?"

"Yes, sir. We are in the eighth and ninth grades now. We love to shoot free throws. That's all we do. Before we came to the ice cream store, we were shooting free throws against four other guys we never met before," Ice Cream stated with a big grin on his face. However, Ice Cream suddenly dropped his head and uttered, "We lost the game. I missed my last free throw."

Coach Blue and his wife encouraged Ice Cream by telling him that he had a bright basketball free throw future ahead of him. The crew continued to tell the coach how often they practiced and what they accomplished at practice. As the conversation continued, the coach informed the crew of an upcoming free throw shooting tournament, followed by a free throw shooting camp in LA. He asked if the young men were interested.

He explained, "I want you fellows to come help teach free throw shooting skills to the younger participants at the camp. However, before the camp, we will start a four-region free throw shooting tournament. You would represent the east team, and I would be your coach. I can talk to your parents about all of this."

Deep replied, "Oh, wow, that sounds great!"

The excitement on the faces of all the teens glowed throughout the ice cream store. By this time, it was late in the day. The boys told the coach they had to get back to Good Pass's house, for their parents were to meet them there. As they left, the coach and his wife informed the crew that it was nice to meet them. He handed each of the other boys a business card so that each parent would have his contact information. The four dream boys and the four smiling girls left the ice cream store and excitedly walked back to the court with the basketballs.

They arrived at 7:15 p.m. and decided to practice for another fifteen minutes before going back to Good Pass's house. The girls again placed their blankets on the ground behind the goal and watched ball after ball soar through the air to the rim. At 7:35 p.m., they stopped shooting free throws and started walking back to Good Pass's house as their parents had told them to be ready at 7:45 p.m. Ice Cream's parents arrived first. After saying, "See you later," to the rest of the crew, he rushed to the car, jumped in the back seat, and immediately spoke of his evening at the ice cream store.

"After we left the court, we went to get ice cream. We were throwing ice cream wrappers into the trash can. A coach from a college from LA saw us. He wants to watch us shoot free throws tomorrow at 4:00 p.m. And if he likes how we shoot, he wants Fats, Range, Deep, and me to go to LA this summer to compete in a free throw shooting tournament, and then he said we could teach young kids how to shoot at a camp. He's willing to be our coach. Coach Blue said when he sees you, he will tell you all about it."

"Oh, that's wonderful, son! We will check into it. But it sounds like it may be okay. Now we will have to go with you," his mother stated.

As the car pulled into the driveway, Ice Cream released his seatbelt, hurriedly got out of the car, and opened his mom's front door and hugged her. He then rushed into the house to call Good Pass.

"I can go! I can go!" he exclaimed as he held the rotary phone to his face.

Good Pass agreed to ask her parents if she could go to LA as well. With a serious look on his face, Fats asked his parents if he could go. On the ride home from Good Pass's house, Deep asked his parents if he could go to LA.

"For what?" exclaimed his father.

Deep then began to explain what had happened at the ice cream store. His father pondered for a few minutes. He then held his hand up with his fingers spread open and looked toward his son. Deep high-fived his father as he received the okay to make the trip. Range also got permission to go to the tournament.

After the boys confirmed that they could go out to California, they informed the girls and asked them to ask their parents. Each of the teens asked their parents about the LA trip and informed them about meeting Coach Blue the following evening. Each household agreed to allow the kids to go as long as each house was represented with a parent. The kids talked back and forth on the telephone that night in anticipation for the trip to Los Angeles.

"I don't believe it, guys. We got to be straight tomorrow. Man, this is so cool. I can't wait," Ice Cream stated.

This type of conversation continued for hours on the phone among the boys. Ice Cream began to see his dream of being a professional free throw shooter coming to life.

Chapter 5

CHURCH ON SUNDAY

The crew had a wonderful Saturday. As Sunday morning rolled around, the crew decided to go to Ice Cream's church. As everyone walked in at eleven o'clock with their families, the choir sang "Order My Steps" for the opening selection. Eventually, everyone took their seats in the congregation and joined in with the choir.

"Oh man, look, look, look. That's Coach Blue. Over there, over there," Block whispered.

"Yes, I see," Ice Cream's mom replied. "We spoke with him last night and told him we would be here. We wanted to surprise you."

Ice Cream and Range smiled and waved at the coach and his wife. Coach Blue nodded with delight to acknowledge the friends. At this point, the team was anxious to get to the basketball court. However, as the choir continued to sing "Order My Steps," Ice Cream paused for a second to think about the true meaning of the song. He pondered for a minute. Ice Cream and the other fellows were used to going to church and hearing good singing and good preaching, but this time, the song meant a little bit more to him. His eyes welled up as he realized the importance of keeping God in his life to lead him.

To him, Coach Blue represented a stepping stone that God placed in his life.

The service continued with the doxology, scripture, and prayer, followed by the morning hymn. Now it was time for the welcome and announcements. The church clerk approached her position, wearing a silver outfit, complimented with a peacock feather in her hat.

"Good morning, church. Do we have any visitors in the house today?" she questioned.

As Coach Blue, his wife, and three other individuals stood up, the congregation applauded.

"On behalf of our pastor and our members, we truly welcome you to this sanctuary today. You could have graced any other church with your presence, but God compelled you to come visit us here on Turnpike Boulevard. Thank you for being here. If you like, please give us your name so our members can be sure to greet you before you leave here today."

Coach Blue introduced himself and his wife and provided the reason for his visit to the church. The other two visitors did the same.

"Once again, we thank you for your visit. Members, don't forget to shake their hands before you exit today. Now for the announcements," the church clerk said. "We do not have too many. We will be fellowshipping with St. Paul's for their ninety-seventh church anniversary on Wednesday night at seven o'clock. I also have a note from the president of the food bank ministry, Sister Hardy. 'Reminder—we will be providing meals on Saturday at eleven thirty. We will also deliver meals as needed.'" The clerk continued with the next announcement. "Oh, bless the Lord!" she exclaimed. "This next announcement is definitely a credit to our young people. Coach Blue spoke to you about his visit today. So let's get these young people up here."

The boys jumped out of their seats, picked up their Bibles, and swiftly walked to the front of the church and stood by the clerk. The youngsters had their basketballs in one hand and their Bibles in the other. The crowd gave cheers of approval to the boys as the coach approached them.

At this point, Coach Blue wanted to go into detail on his visit. "I have been coaching basketball for over twenty years," Coach Blue stated. "And I believe these young fellows are very talented. I believe they have *skills!* For this reason, I am going to watch these guys shoot free throws for thirty minutes to get a good sense of their skills. During that time, I will evaluate different aspects of being a high-percentage free throw shooter. If all goes well today at four o'clock at the court, I hope to see these fellows this summer at the free throw shooting tournament followed by a camp."

"Praise the Lord! Hallelujah!" shouted a man from the rear of the church.

"To God be the glory!" shouted the youth pastor in the pulpit.

Each member of the fantastic four stood proudly as they received words of encouragement from the church members.

"Thank you, Lord, in advance for your blessing!" the clerk cried out.

As she held back the tears, she told the teens to return to their seats; meanwhile, words of praise continued to be sent up. Per the order of service, it was time for the pastor's announcements.

"All right, church. You are now aware of what our young people are doing. Let's get out this evening and support them. Deacon Earl, your television station presented a 'Youth in the Community' piece last year. Check to see if they are willing to come out this afternoon to cover this event. Sister Jones, you are the head cheerleader coach. See if you can get a few members of the squad to come out. And oh, Brother Harold, we could use your help as you cover local sports with the newspaper. I know this is short notice, but I want these young men and the community to know that this church on this corner supports our youth. Our youth are our future. According to Proverbs 22:6, the Word tells us to train up a child in the way he should go, and when he is old, he will not depart from it. So if anyone else has any suggestions about how we can support these boys or any other youth in the community, please, please, please let me know."

As three thirty approached, people started gathering along the court. They were shoulder to shoulder as they conversed and looked toward the north end of the court. The four dream boys were already there, warming up. The four girls were also there, rebounding for the boys. The girls rebounded so many times before for the boys, so it came second nature for them. They knew they had to be on point; they also knew the boys had to be on point. Finally, at three forty-five, the crew decided to get off the court and relax for a few minutes. As they were sitting down, they realized there was a television camera set up and that more people were forming around the court.

"Wow, look at this," Fats said.

Players from the local college basketball team represented their school colors, along with high school students and cheerleaders. The boys and their parents marveled because they had never received this much support from the community before. At three fifty-five, Coach Blue and his wife walked up.

"You ready, fellows?" he asked.

"Yes, Coach! Yes, Coach!" the boys shouted.

The coach did not tell them what or how to shoot. The fellows already decided what they would do. Each player decided to shoot one hundred free throws, with one player on each end of the court. After Deep and Range finished, Ice Cream and Fats shot. The coach intensely watched the youngsters. His wife and he were truly amazed at the talent the boys possessed.

As Ice Cream finish his last fifty free throws, the coach spoke with the boys' parents. He told them he wanted to invest some time in the crew. He informed them he would watch the boys closely throughout their high school careers and would be interested in having the crew play college basketball back in Los Angeles.

However, for now, the coach told the parents, "I want the boys to come to Los Angeles in the summer. I will call each of you tomorrow to give you the details of the tournament and the summer camp. It has been a pleasant meeting you and watching your young men perform."

The parents smiled and informed the coach that they looked forward to hearing from him the following day. So needless to say, the fellows performed great. They had a combined average of a 94 percent success rate at the free throw line.

"Well done!" the coach said as he nodded proudly as the boys walked off the court. Coach Blue told the crew, "I talked with your parents, and it is a *go*."

So after the free throw tryouts and after the coach officially invited the four dream boys to Los Angeles, the crowd's excitement could not be contained. One of the church members was a police officer; he put on his sirens and lights on his black-and-white police cruiser to show support. Good Pass's uncle was an eighteen-wheeler truck driver. He blasted his horn several times, thereby invoking even more excitement. The crowd cheered and jumped and cheered and jumped repeatedly, for they knew the young fellows from their community had just received the opportunity to advance in the sport of free throw shooting.

The television station interviewed the boys at the court that same night as a part of the "Youth in the Community" piece and planned to air it the following morning on the six o'clock news. As the crowd settled down and began to disperse, Ice Cream's pastor extended a prayer to God for his goodness, for his grace, and for the career-starting opportunity he afforded the boys.

"Continue to order their steps, O Lord!" he cried.

Then the crowd joined in. "Amen, amen, amen!"

As the crowd dispersed, tears continued to flow down Ice Cream's cheeks as he watched Coach Blue and his wife leave the court.

Chapter 6

LA, HERE WE COME!

While the months passed slowly, the boys continued to vigilantly practice their free throws to ensure a successful summer in LA. Every day after school, they practiced; whether they practiced alone or with one another, the cycle continued, but each Saturday and Sunday, the peers practiced together. Crowds continued to come out and watch the boys practice and continued to be in awe at their abilities. They always had the young and the old out at the court watching them shot free throws, but ever since the successful performance with Coach Blue, the fellows' popularity had increased.

As they became more known for their abilities within the community, the age of the audience also increased. These boys became the topic of regular conversation at the courts, at the barber, at the church, at school, at family gatherings, and at games. Sports enthusiasts and the occasional basketball watcher alike were blown away by the teens' natural-born talent. It was not uncommon for these followers to ask the boys for their autographs and ask the crew to take pictures with them. The city mayor and the police chief even scheduled a photoshoot with the free throwing crew. The community began to see these inspiring fellows as the true champions they were destined to be.

Eventually, the night before the flight to Los Angeles approached.

"Finally, finally!" Ice Cream declared to his parents. "Tomorrow we leave for the big city. When we are there, we will prove we are the best free throw shooters around."

"Okay, okay, hotshot," his father echoed. "Now get in there and go to bed. We have a long day ahead of us, and we will be getting started early."

"Yes, sir," Ice Cream replied.

"We have an eight-hour plane ride—I think we stop in Charlotte—and three hours' difference."

"Wow, Pop! Good night," he said as he skipped down the hall to his room.

Still, once Ice Cream arrived at his room, instead of going straight to bed, he called the other members of the team.

"This is it. Oh yeah," he whispered to the guys.

Suddenly, he heard a shout from down the once-silent hall.

"Go to bed!"

"Yes, sir," he responded as he swiftly turned off the light and covered himself up with his favorite NBA blanket.

Beep! Beep! Beep! Beep! Beep! Ice Cream was already awake and daydreaming about his professional free throw shooter career.

Twenty minutes later, his elder sister came and knocked on his door. "You better get up. Pop said to make sure you were up."

"Okay," he declared. "It will not take me long to get ready."

Once everyone was dressed, the family sat down at the kitchen table for breakfast. After their mother blessed the table, they talked about the flight timetable and their arrival time in Los Angeles. His father gave the three sisters information concerning the return schedule home. He also gave specific last-minute instructions to the girls to ensure the house was properly taken care of in his absence. The eldest daughter reassured her parents that everything would be in order. Confident in their daughters, the parents nodded.

It was about time to leave for the airport. The prior night, the boys had agreed to call one another right before they departed for the airport.

"We are out!" Ice Cream told Deep.

"Range and Fats already left for the airport," Deep replied.

As the boys hung up the telephones, they excitedly confirmed they would see one another in thirty-five minutes. A block away from the airport, the family saw signs with the boys' names on them. "Go Fats Go!" and "Go Ice Cream Go!" were on two posters. Other signs read "The 4 dream boys head to LA" and "God Bless." Crowds of people stood with signs in their hands as well. "We Love You — Have Fun!"

The words on the signs continued to provide praise and encouragement to the guys. As they entered the airport, there were rows of people from the community with well wishes and high fives. At this time, the fellows were also afforded the opportunity to take pictures and sign more autographs on plain paper, yearbooks, and even basketballs. The community saw these youngsters as the next free throw shooter superstars.

As all this happened, bystanders in the airport wondered what was going on. A few of them stepped forward as the boys autographed basketballs and listened as the boys told everyone how their free throw shooting careers started in the first grade in the back row of a math class. For the people who had never heard the story before, they praised the crew for keeping with their sport and for being so good at such a young age.

"Practice, practice, practice!" Range roared.

Well, the family finally checked their bags and got on the airplane. A few claps rang out from the passengers who had heard the boys' story earlier. The others who did not know of the boys just smiled and whispered to one another about what the boys had achieved. The families took their seats; the flight was uneventful and landed safely and on time in Los Angeles.

Chapter 7

THE TEAMS ARE HERE

When the Virginia gang walked off the plane, they saw Coach Blue waiting for them. The boys' faces lit up like it was Christmas.

"Coach! Coach!" Deep yelled.

"Hi, fellows. Welcome to LA. Everything go okay on the trip?"

Ice Cream's father replied, "Yes."

Everyone else smiled in agreement as they walked to pick up their luggage. As they departed the building, the coach informed them that the van was across the way in short-term parking. After a brief walk, everyone loaded their gear in the van. The coach then began to update the families concerning the hotel arrangements and the upcoming week's events.

"Girls, I have you in one hotel room. The boys are in another one together. All the parents have their separate hotel rooms, and two of the parents' rooms are connected to the kids'," he explained.

He further told them that after the seven nights in the hotel, the girls would be staying in the girls' dorm at the university, and the boys would be in the boys' dorm. The coach continued by saying that after one week, each family would be responsible for their own hotel arrangements. Each family stated that this was fine.

"Thank you so much," Fats's mother added. "It is pretty awesome that the foundation agreed to pay as much as they did to accommodate us for a whole week in a nice hotel."

Ice Cream's mother joined in the conversation. "Yes, God sure does answer prayer. Who would imagine we would be here in the big city with our kids? Oh, this is such a blessing."

As the conversation continued, Range and Block were awed by the lights and the city life of LA. The coach was amused as he confirmed there was a lot going on in LA. Set Shot's father noticed the price of gas; Ice Cream showed a lot of interest in the fast, pretty cars. Each person was fascinated in his or her own way with the environment of the California city.

When they arrived at the hotel, everyone dismounted and headed to check in. They were each quiet, tired from the all-day trip from Virginia. Therefore, after checking in, they went to their designated hotel rooms. Of course, the youngsters were tired, but they were very excited. Their parents informed them not to leave the hotel until everyone got back together later that evening for supper. After Coach made sure there were no issues and everyone was secured in their hotel room, he spoke with the crew and reinforced to them that practice would start bright and early Monday morning at six thirty. He also reminded them of the time for the free throw tournament.

"Fellows, you have four days. Be ready!" the coach barked.

As the coach left, the crew yelled, "Yes, sir!"

Range followed up with "We'll be ready, Coach!"

As the evening rolled around, the boys knew tomorrow was their day to really impress the coach. They wanted to show the coach that they were not only great free throw shooters but also excellent athletes.

At five thirty the following morning, the alarm clock rang.

"Already . . ." Deep murmured as he slapped the alarm clock.

"Get up, man. Get up, get up, get up!" Ice Cream said. Ice Cream had been up since four forty-five; he could not contain his excitement.

The boys got up, showered quickly, and ate some fruit cocktail and turkey sandwich meat their parents had put in the compact refrigerator for them.

"Okay, I'm ready to go," Deep said.

"Come on, guys. Let's pray before we leave. God is ordering our steps. And I am so thankful," Ice Cream tearfully requested.

After finishing the prayer, each of the dream boys called his parents to let them know they were headed downstairs to meet Coach Blue.

As Ice Cream talked to his dad, he heard, "Be safe. Follow the rules and regulations the coach gives you."

"Yes, sir," he replied.

The boys eagerly jumped on the elevator and headed down to the lobby to meet the coach.

"We made it on time," Deep said.

"Yes, we did." Range giggled as he shook his head, smiling at Deep.

"Man, stop playing." Deep chuckled.

Then they noticed Coach Blue walking into the hotel. They ran up and greeted him good morning and dashed off to the van. Once arriving at the university, the boys couldn't believe their eyes—the University of Southern California (USC) dorm.

"Wow!" Deep shouted. "This is nice, Coach."

Coach Blue encouraged them. "Glad you like it, son. This is just the beginning. Listen to what I tell you. Practice and work hard on the court and off the court and continue in your faith. And you guys should be just fine."

The coach then showed them to the locker room and then told them to be out on the track in ten minutes. When they got out to the track, Fats led the ten-minute warmup and then informed the coach they were finished.

"Okay, guys, let's see what you got. I want you to work hard and knock out two miles for me around this track. Now that's eight times around, again eight times around. Don't short-change me," the coach demanded.

"Coach, we got this!" Fats roared.

The boys knew they were going to be timed for the two-mile run; they knew the coach wanted them to run the first mile in around six minutes and forty-five seconds.

Standing at the white painted starting line on the track, the boys echoed, "We got this! We got this! We got this!"

Then they heard the coach yell, "Ready, set, go!"

They took off. The coach attentively observed each member of the team as they swiftly ran around the track. He perceived the boys were pushing one another; they tended to stay in a pack. He liked the team approach he noticed with these boys despite their young age. As the boys rounded the last lap, he showed much delight as he challenged them to give a little bit more. One by one, as they approached the line, each youngster realized he finished within the time Coach Blue had set.

"Walk it off. Walk it off, fellows. Excellent job. Walk it off," he directed them.

Though tired, the boys chatted and patted one another on their backs as they proudly walked up to the gym for weight training. Once again, they chanted softly, "We got this. We got this, man."

Well, the crew finished their first workout session with Coach Blue. They were very pleased with the events of the morning. Before going back to the hotel, they showered and then stopped by the university cafeteria and ate breakfast. Once they arrived back at the hotel, they all sat in the lobby to discuss the upcoming schedules. The coach informed them that on Tuesday morning, the workout would be similar.

"No problem, Coach!" Fats sang out.

Shortly after the coach and the fellows got back to the hotel, the girls and the parents came downstairs to go to the hotel restaurant to get some lunch. Everyone greeted one another. At this time, the coach also took this opportunity to update the parents. He answered additional questions about scheduling and the welfare of the youngsters. Each parent acknowledged what the coach had told them and showed much appreciation for all Coach Blue was doing to assist them. Coach Blue told them he would come back at three o'clock to show them the university and where they would stay once they left the hotel. He bade them good afternoon and left to return home.

The families went to eat lunch and shared with the boys how proud they were of them. The dream boys were not hungry, for they had just eaten breakfast, so they talked about the morning practice with the rest of the family. After lunch, everyone went back up to the hotel rooms. The boys took naps; the parents watched television, but the girls decided to go back down to the lobby and watch the cycling competition. At two fifty-five, everyone was in the lobby, waiting on the coach. Good Pass's father told the kids to go stand outside and inform them when the coach arrived at the hotel. He and his wife arrived promptly at three o'clock. Everyone jumped in the van and headed out for an afternoon on the town.

The Blues turned out to be excellent tour guides. The families saw the university where the free throw shooting event would be held. They saw the Hollywood sign on Mount Lee, the Hollywood Walk of Fame, and Muscle Beach. With all the sightseeing, around six o'clock, they decided to eat out for dinner. Mrs. Blue suggested Nick + Stef's Steakhouse. The meal was delicious. Everyone was quite pleased with the evening. By eight fifteen, they returned to the hotel to relax. Once again, they thanked the coach and his wife for their support and went into the lobby. There, they noticed a baseball game on the television. Everyone decided to stay in the lounge and watch the game. After the game ended, the parents went back upstairs to their rooms. They told the crew to be back up in their rooms by ten o'clock. As they walked, they spoke of the long relationship the boys had with one another and with the girls ever since the first grade. They spoke of the respect each child showed one another as well as each parent. They spoke of God's grace to each family. They spoke of their blessings.

On Tuesday morning, all the boys jumped up again to go to practice except for Deep.

"It's time to get up already?" he slurred as he wiped the sleep from his eyes.

Fats tossed a pillow at Deep, and Range grabbed Deep's leg.

"I'm up, I'm up!" Deep playfully shouted.

So once again, after getting ready and after having prayer, the team raced down to the lobby to meet the coach. Coach Blue picked them up, and they went directly to the gym, but this time, when they arrived, the coach had a little surprise for them. Coach Blue called his rebound staff, who were sports medicine majors, to assist with the practice. So after the warmup and a one-mile run, the boys began shooting free throws.

They shot close to three hundred free throw shots each with their rebounders in place. Each shooter and rebounder discussed the rebounder's position on the court and how the shooter would like the ball returned. Ice Cream preferred the ball to be returned as a zip pass with no bounce at chest level. Range liked the ball returned from the rebounder with one bounce. The team spent hours on the relationship with the rebounder, for they knew the importance of a good setup for the next free throw shot. They diligently practiced just as they were competing. The entire crew was determined to have a victorious weekend.

After an excellent day of practice, Coach Blue returned the crew to the hotel and, at that time, spoke with the parents, for he constantly kept them updated as to the ongoing schedule. Ice Cream's mother told the coach that the other competitors were staying at the same hotel.

The coach smiled and responded, "Yes, I am aware of that. As a matter of fact, I meet with the other coaches as well as the team members and parents tonight at six o'clock to make sure everyone is ready for Friday evening. This is really a special time for all these young men. I am always very excited for them. This event can truly be a life-changing factor. There is so much talent here, and each year, I see dozens of these young fellow trying to improve themselves by using their hands with that very basketball Ice Cream and Fats are holding right now."

"Well, we are so thankful for the boys to have this opportunity," Fats's mother replied.

His father additionally thanked God for the blessing. The coach finished the conversation and reminded them of the evening meeting. He also reminded them that they would go to the mall on Thursday evening to pick up the uniforms that were ordered for the free throw competition.

Suddenly, they heard, "Man, you better get out of my face! I ain't playing with you!"

"Save it for the court. Save it for the court," one of the members of the west team responded.

"What's going on over there?" Range asked.

The members of the opposing teams were getting into a heated conversation. Coach Blue called the other coaches of the teams to inform them about the incident. By the time the coaches returned to the restaurant, the hotel management had defueled the situation.

Range's mother shook her head in disappointment and said, "Wow, that is terrible. Guys and ladies, always show respect in whatever you do. I'm telling you what my mother used to tell me. 'Do unto others as you have them do unto you.' God is a good God, and he doesn't want us to act in that manner. Remember, *love* is the greatest commandment."

Both the boys and the girls nodded and verbalized their agreement.

"Now let's really show them boys who the real champs will be Friday, and we will back it up on Saturday!" she roared with a childish smile.

"We got this! We got this! We got this!" each boy echoed.

Later that evening, the families decided they want to see what else LA had to offer. Ice Cream wanted to check out the specialty indoor car lot; Range and Deep were interested in the Ripley's Believe It or Not! museum.

"I have a great idea!" Fats said. "The casino is right down the street. I have an extra $1.27."

"Boy, is that your tithe money?" his father questioned as he chuckled.

"I know what I'm going to do when we get back—go to the pool," Dunk added.

As the evening went on, they all enjoyed themselves. When they returned to the hotel, Fats reminded everyone that they missed the casino.

Wednesday's morning practice started a little later. So the families had an early start and decided to have breakfast together.

"Wow, there're a lot of people here," Ice Cream stated as he observed an elderly couple slowly walking to their seats with a tray full of grits and shrimp.

"Hey, guys, stay focused and show some manners," his mother responded.

Immediately afterward, Fats and Deep said, "Look over there, y'all."

After Tuesday's episode, the crew realized the other free throw region teams from the north, south, and west were also staying at the same hotel. So once again, the crew found themselves in the midst of the other team. The members of the teams watched one another as they recognized the competition. The other teams' members were a few years older than the east region team, but the young men were in no way intimidated. Therefore, after breakfast, the families proudly left and went into the lobby, talked for a little while, and then decided to return to their rooms. By this time, it was time for Coach Blue to pick up the team.

At practice, the team started with just a half-mile warm up. After the short jog, the coach rounded the youngsters up.

"Okay, fellows. I know you have skills, and I know you are in excellent shape. So we are going to continue to work on techniques and your relationship with your rebounders."

They practiced and practiced passing, stances, ball releases, and follow-through techniques. They knew it was, as they say, "the little things" that would make or break them during the competition. The boys worked hard, and they felt very good about themselves.

"Ice Cream, you good, boy!" Range giggled. "But I'm better." He smirked.

"Keep working with it." Fats laughed.

By the end of the day, all the coaches and their staff arrived to have a meeting with the team members to go over the tournament rules and regulations. The meeting went smoothly, and the boys seemed to understand what was expected of them during the competition. After they took care of official business with the players, the coaches and the staff had some final preparations for Friday's tournament; thus, they stayed in the conference room, but it was time for dinner for everyone else. So the teams assembled in the restaurant.

Once again, the food looked delicious as there was a buffet-style corner and a menu for those who desired it. The evening went smoothly until Ice Cream decided he wanted some ice cream. He sprang from his chair and headed toward the freezer box. At the same time, the captain for the west team left his table to get some blueberries. As they stood at the counter, Ice Cream asked the west captain how long he had been shooting free throws.

"A few years. What about you?" he responded.

"Since I was in the first grade," Ice Cream proudly stated with a smile on his face.

"Snap!" he responded. "Wow, that's amazing. Looks like we got some competition. By the way, I'm Jerome."

The members of the other teams saw Ice Cream and Jerome talking. The captains of the south and north teams immediately did not like the relationship the two boys were forming. They conjured up a plan. One captain decided to trip Ice Cream, and the other tripped Jerome as they walked back to their seats. That was the ignition the boys needed to start a fight.

"Stop! Stop!" Block's mom yelled.

She and Fats's mom were the only parents left downstairs at this point, and they could not contain the boys. The staff in the restaurant called hotel management and reported the incident and asked for help. The security arrived promptly to see the ongoing fight. They blew their whistles and barked out orders for them to stop. The boys continued to throw punches; eventually, they had to physically separate the boys. Security then gathered and took the four captains to the management office.

At the same time, Block's mom called Coach Blue to inform him of the situation. "You all have to rush back over here right now," she ordered.

"What's wrong? What happened? Is everyone okay?" he gasped.

"Ice Cream and three other boys were fighting in the restaurant," she responded.

"Okay, we are still in the hotel in the conference room. We will be there directly." He sighed.

When the coaches arrived, they saw the other twelve boys quietly sitting in the lounge. The look on the youngsters' faces was as if the world was coming to an end. The coaches entered the office where the boys were held. They were quite upset with each player as they had just had a conversation with them per the dos and don'ts. Coach Blue looked directly at Ice Cream. Ice Cream glared off into space, for he knew he had disappointed the coach and his family. Not one boy engaged in eye contact with any of the coaches as they knew what had just happened was totally unacceptable. After this tense moment, security described to the coaches the situation and what had occurred. The coaches listened attentively to what the captains had to add. After a brief conversation among the coaches, they decided to suspend all four boys from the first two rounds of the tournament on Friday night.

Unfortunately, this incident couldn't stay among the coaches; this violation had to be reported to the tournament board. It was therefore agreed to by hotel security and the tournament board that the captains had to also be supervised whenever they were in the hotel. Coach Blue spoke with the players and their parents as to what this meant; they decided to keep the problem in house.

"Okay, fellows, since you have a lot of energy, we will hit the gym to practice. This incident is quite disturbing, but we still have a tournament to win. Get your gear, and let's hit the courts," commanded Coach Blue. "Suicides, wind sprints, pushups—get ready!" he barked.

While the boys retrieved their gear, the coach spoke with the parents and security about the issue. Coach followed with "This will all work out. I know Ice Cream is a good young man—with the key word being 'young.' We will hit practice hard, and I will bring them back here to the hotel. Tomorrow we will have a light practice and take care of other business."

The team returned from their hotel room, and everyone was ready to depart to the gym.

"Hey, guys, let's go. Needless to say, I am truly disappointed. Are you ready for practice?" the coach asked.

"Yes, sir," they replied.

"We will hold it down," Deep replied.

Ice Cream then stated, "Okay, y'all, shoot good free throws."

At this point, the coach followed with "Son, be good, and you will return to shooting."

As they walked out the door, Coach Blue told security that Ice Cream was in good hands. The team jumped in the van to head to practice. During the entire trip to the university, they talked about what to expect on Friday evening. They were slowly realigning their emotional states.

When Thursday morning came around, the boys decided to get up early for a little run. They were determined to stay in shape.

As they approached the elevator, Ice Cream explained, "We practiced hard all week, and I want to make sure we stay good."

"For sure, bro!" Fats said as he was running down the long hall toward the elevator.

After the dream boys finished their aerobic workout, they returned to the hotel and informed Deep's mom that they were safely back. His mom told them what a great job they were doing and continued to encourage them by stating that the coach would be very proud of them.

Coach Blue picked them up that morning for a light practice with the rebounders. They were instructed to warm up and run around the court four times. After that, the coach told them to get with their rebounders and put up one hundred free throw shots.

"Concentrate now. Pay attention to how you receive the ball. Watch your technique," he directed.

After they finished, they huddled together, high-fived, and bear-hugged one another.

"What you think, Coach?" Ice Cream questioned.

"I love it, fellows. Excellent workout," he responded.

On the way back to the hotel, the coach started talking about the tournament.

"Hi, guys. We have to win the first two rounds to advance to the third round."

Fats inquired, "When will Ice Cream be back with us?"

They were informed that Ice Cream, along with the other captains, would rejoin the teams at the third round.

"And, boys, eat good and get plenty of rest tonight," the coach order them.

"We there, Coach. We there," Fats said.

"Breakfast time—yes, yes, yes!" Deep said.

"Didn't you eat two sandwiches right after we ran?" Range asked.

Deep looked at him and responded, "Sure did, but I worked out hard, and I gotta eat. Stop playing."

Upon arriving back at the hotel breakfast area, they immediately noticed the north team eating as well as the south team heading to the university for practice. The youngsters presented their meal vouchers, ordered their food, and sat down about four booths away from the north team. The boys felt a little uncomfortable and somewhat puzzled as they noticed the other team members laughing and peeking toward them.

"I am not getting in any more trouble, guys," Ice Cream said. "I know what Coach told me. Pop wasn't too happy about that mess last night either," he continued with a look of despair on his face.

"Yes, the coach said to stay focused. We don't have time for this," Deep added.

"Oh, Ice Cream, you have lockdown anyway. Security is over there looking at you right now," Fats quickly joked.

Then they heard, "They will not outshoot us on Friday."

"Nor Saturday," another team member added.

Fats and the other guys did not respond; they continued to eat their breakfast. Shortly after that, the west team went to the breakfast area and ordered their food. Then just as the morning news was coming on, the girls and the parents arrived for breakfast. As they were walking in, the local news channel caught their attention.

A manly voice projected from the television set, "In just one day, the free throw tournament at USC will begin at six o'clock in the evening. This tournament has been a yearly event for over twenty years. Some of the best basketball players and free throw shooters will be here. Of course, there will be scouts from high schools and colleges to meet these young men. Also, on a side note, Coach Blue informed us that a tournament for girls is in the works. The program is targeted to be up and running next year."

The sports anchor continued and mentioned each coach, team, and captain by name. Cheers fanned out throughout the room.

"I'm ready! I'm ready!" Range proclaimed.

Everyone was excited about the upcoming weekend and wanted to keep the excitement going.

"Hey, guys, we haven't been to the pool since Tuesday night. What you think?" Deep asked.

Good Pass and Dunk were ready to go before Deep could finish the question.

Dunk followed with bragging rights. "I've been swimming since I was like five years old. My sister's best friend is a lifeguard at the community center. I want to do that when I'm old enough."

"That sounds great, but you know what I want to do," Deep responded as he high-fived the rest of the team.

Dunk smartly replied, "No, tell us."

Fats interrupted. "This is great! I am having so much fun. Oh man, this is it. Tonight we go to the mall to check out some gear."

"But Coach already has our uniforms for the tournament, so we are good," Range replied.

"Range, you know I love the mall." Fats giggled.

"And don't forget, guys. We have church on Sunday. After that, on Monday, bright and early, we start the summer camp. Man, we are gonna be busy," Ice Cream added.

Set Shot and the other girls just smiled and laughed at the four dream boys.

"Look at them," Block said, nodding in delight.

"One thing at a time, guys. We gotta win this tournament first," Deep expressed.

"True that," Block added.

Thus, the kids finished off their afternoon with a relaxing session at the pool.

As the evening approached, Coach Blue arrived to take the young people to the mall to gather their uniforms. Walking around the mall turned out to be quite an outing for the team and the young ladies. They made a little shopping trip out of it. Set Shot bought some new tennis shoes; Dunk purchased another bathing suit to add to her seven-suit collection. The others did more window shopping and eating soft pretzels with ice cream than anything. The coach informed them it was time to head back to the hotel.

Chapter 8

THE FREE THROW TOURNAMENT
SHOOTOUT

"Hey, man, it's 3:30 p.m. Let's start gearing up!" Ice Cream was fired up about this free throw tournament.

"And you know that!" Deep uttered very loudly.

"Hey, man, let's do this!" Fats and Range were steamed up as well.

The dream boys were ready, looking good in their all-white uniforms with their names in purple letters on the back. They all met downstairs in the main lobby.

"Wow, wow! You guys look great!" The parents and the girls were elated.

"Thank you, thank you," the dream boys responded.

The rebounders were looking good as well.

"Hey, look! Coach Blue coming in!" Ice Cream mentioned.

"Hello, hello," Coach Blue and his wife said.

"You ready to shoot, guys?" Coach asked.

"Yes, sir! Yes, sir!" The boys were juiced up, clapping their hands.

"Let's get on the bus, everybody," Coach Blue said, steamed up as well.

The north, west, and south teams had left earlier to head to the LA Forum. While Coach Blue and his team plus the crew were riding, it was very silent.

"Hey, guys, continue to stay focused," Coach stated.

When they arrived at the LA Forum, it was packed.

"Hey, guys—and my male rebounders—let's head to the locker room," Coach Blue ordered.

The four young fellows zoomed past everybody, running, fired up.

"Slow down! Slow down!" Coach Blue and the parents shouted out.

"Okay, you four women rebounders, head to the arena and wait for us," Coach Blue said to his female rebounders.

"Okay, Coach!" they answered.

At 6:00 p.m., all four teams came out to the court to warm up. The north and south teams started their free throw warmup first. The east and west teams were seated until their time.

"Hey, Coach Blue, those guys are good," Fats voiced out.

"You just stay focused, Fats," Coach Blue stated to him.

After the north and south teams finished their ten-minute warmup, the east and west teams exited to the court at around 6:30 p.m. for their ten-minute warmup.

"Hey, man, let's do this!" Ice Cream blurted out.

"Yes, sir! Yes, sir!" Deep was fired up.

The fans were looking at and studying these free throws plus taking pictures. The game horn sounded off to start the tournament. The referee called each team captain to center court to toss the coin and see which two teams would start the first round. It was the south team versus the west team to start. Ice Cream and the other three captains would not shoot in the first round because of the fight at the hotel.

"Man, it's not just going to be right without Ice Cream," Fats voiced out.

"I know, man," Range and Deep responded.

"Look at the girls—they look sad too," Fats stated.

"Hey, fellows, at halftime, let's go back inside the locker room to relax our minds."

"Okay, Coach Blue," the dream boys responded.

The south and west teams started their first free throw shooters at the line to begin the first quarter. Both shooters were shooting very well in the first quarter. The south team was leading by two points all the way to the end of the first quarter. Going into the second quarter, the second free throw shooters for the south and west teams were shooting and also doing great. By the end of the second quarter, the south team had a ten-point lead at halftime.

"Okay, guys, it's time to head to the locker room to get ready for our game," Coach Blue declared.

"Let's go, fellows!" Ice Cream voiced out.

The fantastic four zipped up from their seats and rushed to the locker room with Coach Blue. The north team exited to their locker room as well. The third quarter started, and the west team came back to take the lead by four points with two minutes left in the third quarter. The south team had come back to tie the score at the sound of the horn to end the third quarter. While the dream boys were getting ready for their game, Coach Blue stepped out for a minute to see what was going on with the south-and-west game. The dream boys rushed to get dressed, looking for Coach Blue to return.

"Hey, Coach Blue, who leading the south-and-west game?" Deep voiced out.

"Son, do not worry about their game. Stay focused on your game next," Coach Blue declared.

At the start of the fourth quarter, the first free throw shooters for the south and west teams had to shoot again to fill in for the captains. All the captains couldn't shoot until the third or fourth round of the tournament. The final quarter was on the way. Both free throw shooters were doing very well almost the whole time. With three minutes left, the south team was leading by two points. With less than one minute left, the west team came to tie the game with ten seconds left; the game went into overtime. The second free throw shooters for both teams started shooting in the overtime period. The west team was leading by two points with one minute left to play. Everybody started standing up, cheering for their team, with thirty-five seconds left to play. With two seconds to shoot, the free throw shooter for the south team made the last free throw shot at the buzzer to win the game.

Coach Blue and his east team, waiting in the hallway, were ready to exit to the court. The north team was waiting on their side of the hallway as well. The south team came to a victory over the west team to win their first round of the tournament. They could relax for two games. The west team had to play against the loser of the east-and-north game.

After the south and west teams had cleared the court, it was time for the north team and Coach Blue's east team to come out and warm up their free throws. As the east team approached the court, their fans started shouting and cheering loud for them.

"Let's go, fellows! Let's go, fellows! Let's go, fellows!" the four supporting girls shouted out.

It seemed like more fans were clapping and cheering for the east team because of the fantastic dream boys' free throw shooting skills since the first grade.

Ice Cream noticed his teammates' concentration. "Good warmup shooting, guys!"

The fantastic dream boys seemed to be ready for this game, and their rebounders were throwing great zip chest passes to them.

"Good chest pass, man!" Range shouted out in warmups.

The game horn sounded off, and both teams rushed to their benches.

"Okay, guys, this is it. Let's stay focused and make good free throw shots," Coach Blue declared to them. "Fats, you will start first," Coach Blue ordered.

"We can do it! We can do this, Coach!" Deep shouted out.

"Okay, guys, let's pray," Coach Blue demanded.

After the prayer, the game horn sounded off. Fats and the first free throw shooter for the north team started for the first quarter of the second round game.

"Yes, sir, Fats!" Coach Blue blasted out.

The north shooter was shooting great also with two minutes left in the first quarter. The game was tied, and the crowd was making very loud cheers. Down with five seconds left, the north team was leading by three points. The first quarter was over. Back to the bench went Fats and the first shooter for the north team.

"Okay, guys, we are only down three points," Coach Blue stated. "Okay, Range, it's your turn to shoot in the second quarter."

The buzzer sounded off to start the second quarter. Range and the second shooter for the north team approached their free throw line.

"Come on, Range, put the ball in the basket!" Ice Cream was steamed up.

After Ice Cream spoke out to Range, he started gunning free throws one behind the other. The second free throw shooter for the north team was doing great as well. By the end of the second quarter, also the halftime period, the east team was leading by eight points.

"Way to come back, guys!" Coach Blue blasted out in the locker room. "Okay, guys, continue to stay focused at the free throw line. Deep, you will start the third quarter."

"Okay, Coach Blue. I am ready," Deep voiced out.

Both teams headed back to the court for their eight-minute warmup before the third quarter start. The buzzer sounded off again; both teams rushed to their benches.

"Okay, guys, let's maintain and shoot good free throws," Coach Blue voiced to his team during the huddle.

The buzzer sounded off again. Deep and the third shooter approached their free throw line to start the third quarter. Deep was shooting very well the whole time with two minutes left in the third quarter, and the north team was down by four points.

"Yes, sir, Deep!" Ice Cream shouted out.

With two seconds left, the east team was still leading by one point.

As the third quarter came to the end, the fans were shouting, "We want Ice Cream! We want Ice Cream!" Ice Cream couldn't shoot until the next round.

At the beginning of the fourth quarter, Fats had to shoot again with the first shooter for the north team. Fats was shooting very great, and the shooter for the north team was a little off the mark while shooting his shots. The east team was leading by eight points under six minutes left in the fourth quarter. The north team made a strong comeback.

"Oh no! The north team is leading by four points!" Ice Cream shouted out.

"Time out! Time out!" Coach Blue shouted to the referee. "Fats, you have to stay focused on your follow-through shot, son," Coach Blue instructed in the huddle.

After the period was over, everybody started cheering very loudly. Fats and the north team shooter started back shooting with forty-five seconds left to play. Ice Cream was looking very serious at Fats shooting his free throw shots.

"All right! All right! All right, Fats!" Coach Blue shouted out.

The east team was back in the lead by two points with ten seconds left to play. In the last seven seconds, the north team made the last two free throws. Fats made his last two free throws at the same time to put his team with a two-point lead at the final buzzer.

"Yes, sir! Yes, sir! Yes, sir, Fats!" Ice Cream shouted out, jumping up and down and off the bench along with his teammates.

Everybody from the east team rushed to the court, hugging and cheering one another.

"I can shoot in the championship round against the south team!"

"Yes, sir!" Ice Cream was delighted, with his arms open wide.

All the sports reporters started interviewing Coach Blue and his fantastic four right there, courtside. The whole state of Virginia back home saw this great game on their local television station. After everything was over courtside, Coach Blue and his dream team headed back to the locker room to get dressed.

"Great game. Great game, guys. What a great comeback!" Coach Blue said to his team. "Ice Cream, you will shoot with us on Saturday night, the championship game against the great south team."

"Ice Cream is back! Ice Cream is back! Ice Cream is back!" his teammates shouted, jumping for joy in the locker room.

The parents and the crew were waiting out in the hallway for them to come out to head back to the hotel. When the dream boys and Coach Blue arrived in the hallway, lots of cheers were going on as they headed to the bus. While they were riding back to the hotel, it was continuing joy all the way back.

"Okay, guys, great game tonight," Coach Blue declared when they all entered the main lobby.

"Coach, we came back fast in that last quarter," Range asserted.

"Yes, we did, Range," Coach Blue responded. "Hey, listen up, everybody. My wife and I will be back here tomorrow evening at five o'clock to pick all of you up."

"Okay, Coach Blue," they all responded to him.

It was very late that night, and they all departed from one another to get ready for bed. The fantastic four entered their room and rested for a minute.

"Hey, man, let's shoot some paper balls in the trash can before we go to sleep," Ice Cream announced.

"Okay, man," Fats, Range, and Deep answered.

The dream boys practiced for a half hour and then went to bed.

Early Saturday morning, the boys got out of their beds at nine o'clock, got dressed, and headed downstairs to eat breakfast. They noticed the south team free throw shooters were there as well.

"Good luck at the game tonight," the south team free throw boys expressed to the fantastic four.

"Thank you!" the dream boys responded.

"I heard those east team boys can shoot free throws real good," the south team boys whispered to one another.

"They are not going to outshoot us tonight!" one of the south team boys shouted out very loudly.

"Did you hear that, Ice Cream?" Fats, Range, and Deep mumbled.

"Yeah, man. Remember, guys, stay focused, like Coach told us."

"You are right, man," Deep responded.

While the dream boys were preparing their food to eat at their table, both teams were putting fear in one another's hearts for tonight's game. At 11:00 a.m., the parents and girls for both teams approached the breakfast lobby to join their team and eat as well. Everybody was talking softly while eating their breakfast.

"Look, man, what's on television!"

"They are talking about the championship game tonight," Fats mumbled softly.

"Yeah, man," the dream boys mumbled to one another.

"Hey, guys, keep it down, okay?" the parents voiced.

"Okay," the boys answered.

The sports reporters were talking on television about how this would be the greatest free throw championship game and how Coach Blue's east team were great free throw shooters. The south team really did not want to hear that comment.

"That's okay, guys. We will win tonight," one of the south team shooters declared to his teammates.

"It's now 1:00 p.m. We must head back to our rooms and rest to get ready to meet Coach Blue at the main lobby by 6:00 p.m.," the parents announced.

Ice Cream and his teammates walked the girls to their room door.

"We will meet you all right here outside this door at 5:30 p.m.," Range voiced out.

"Okay, guys," Set Shot answered for the girls.

When the fantastic four arrived at their room, they just rested on their beds, holding their basketballs, thinking about tonight's game.

"Hey, man, it is 4:30 p.m. Time to change into our uniforms," Deep asserted.

"Let's go, fellows!" Fats zipped up from his bed.

The parents and the girls were getting ready as well. "Everybody ready?" Ice Cream voiced out to his teammates. "Let's pray."

The girls and the parents did the same in their rooms. After all the prayers, it was game time. The dream boys exited and headed to the girls' room door at 5:30 p.m. *Knock! Knock!* Ice Cream banged heavily on the girls' door. The girls came to meet them.

The girls came out with "You guys look great."

"Thank you," the boys responded.

They all headed downstairs to meet the parents at 6:00 p.m.

"Wow, you guys look great!" the parents voiced out to the boys.

"Thank you, thank you," the dream boys responded.

They all sat down, waiting for Coach Blue and his wife to arrive. The north, west, and south teams, along with their crew, came down as well to leave with their coaches. It was very silent at that moment. Four big buses were waiting outside to load the teams. There were two free throw games playing tonight. The first game would determine which team would place third or fourth place. That would either be the north or west team. The second game would determine which team would place first or second place. That would be either the east or south team.

"Good evening, my crew," Coach Blue and his wife and the rebounders voiced to the crew.

"Good evening, Coach Blue and Mrs. Blue and rebounders!" the dream boys and the girls plus the parents responded.

All the teams started loading onto their individual buses and headed to the arena.

Coach Blue was walking back and forth on their bus, talking to his dream boys. "Hey, fellows, we have to shoot good free throws tonight, and my rebounders have to throw great passes."

"Yes, sir!" they all voiced out.

"This will be the order of shooting—Fats, Range, Deep, and Ice Cream," Coach Blue declared. "My rebounding team lineup will be Team 2, Team 4, Team 6, and Team 8."

When the four buses arrived at the arena, they had a private parking area in the parking garage. All the teams had their own pathways to their locker rooms. The north-and-west game was scheduled at 7:30 p.m., and the east-and-south game would follow next. The four teams were in their locker rooms, getting prepared for the final tournament rounds. All the parents and girls from each team exited inside the arena courtside, sitting in. Coach Blue's male rebounders were in the locker room with the team, and his female rebounders were courtside, sitting with the parents and girls. The time had arrived for the north and west teams to exit onto the court for their free throw warmup. The east and south teams were coming out of their locker rooms to be seated and watch the first game with their crew.

"Hey, Coach Blue, this will be a good free throw game," Deep voiced.

"It will be, son," Coach Blue responded.

The game horn sounded off to start the game. The north team was leading by six points at halftime.

"Hey, Coach Blue, this is a nice halftime show," Ice Cream asserted. "Wow! These guys can play those drums great."

"I see them, Cream. They are great," Coach Blue responded.

Late in the third quarter, the west team came back to lead by four points with three minutes and twenty-nine seconds left in the quarter. By the end of the third quarter, the west team raised a great lead by fifteen points. The fourth quarter was on the way, and the north team jumped back quickly with a ten-point lead with twenty-five seconds left. It was not enough time for the west team to come back. The game horn sounded off, and the north team won the game. That made the north team place third and the west team place fourth for their game status.

Now this was the moment everybody had been waiting for—the championship game. After the court was cleared from the previous game, the east and south teams approached the court to warm up their free throw shots.

"Looking great, guys!" Coach Blue was watching his fantastic four shooting their free throws.

The game sounded off, ready for the first quarter. The dream boys rushed back to Coach Blue's bench for instructions on what to do at the free throw line. Fans were cheering for the east team as well as for the south team. Some fans recognized the fantastic four a while back, shooting 97 percent at a young age.

"Hey, Joe! That's Ice Cream right there!"

"He is great at the line!" he voiced to his friend behind Coach Blue's bench.

Coach Blue overheard the comment. "Hey, guys, we have some fans sitting right behind us. Let's shoot great free throws," Coach Blue mumbled softly to his dream boys.

"Okay, Coach!" The fantastic four gave one another high fives.

The game horn sounded off to play. Fats was first along with the first shooter for the south team to approach their free throw line. Both teams started out shooting very well.

"All right, Fats!" Coach Blue shouted out.

"Way to go, Fats!" his teammates voiced out as well.

By the end of the first quarter, the east team was leading by one point. The start of the second quarter was on the way. Range and the second shooter for the south team were shooting.

"Yes, sir, Range!" Ice Cream shouted out.

"I believe we will win this game, Coach," Deep voiced out.

"I hope so, Deep," Coach Blue responded.

The south team tried to take the lead but could not do it by halftime. The east team was up six points, plus the fans were into this game, cheering the whole first half of the game.

"Good! Good! Good, fellows!" Coach Blue shouted out in the locker room. "Let's finish this third and fourth quarter with the championship trophy, guys!"

"Yes, sir, Coach!" the dream boys responded.

They were steamed up on their way out of the locker room and back to the court. Both teams were on the court warming up before the third quarter began. The game horn sounded off, and the teams rushed to their benches.

"Okay, Fats, you are on," Coach Blue directed in the huddle.

"Yes, sir. Let's do this!" Deep shouted out in the huddle.

When the game horn sounded off again, Deep and the third shooter for the south team approached their free throw line to start shooting. Both shooters were shooting very great from the line.

"Yeah, Deep!" Fats blurted out.

The parents and the girls were getting their cheers on as well. The south team was down no more than eight points throughout the whole first half and most of the third quarter as well. Now they were leading by four points by the end of the third quarter.

"What happened, Deep? Your follow-through was a little off." Coach Blue was confused in the huddle.

Deep came to a silence with his head hanging down and headed to sit down on the bench.

"Okay, Ice Cream. It's on you, son. Bring it home for us," Coach Blue declared.

The game horn sounded off, so Ice Cream and the last shooter for the south team approached their free throw line, ready to shoot.

"Let's go, Cream!" Good Pass and Coach Blue shouted out.

They started out shooting great on both ends. With three minutes left to play in the championship game, it was a battle with these last two shooters all the way out. They were knocking down free throws one after another easy. The game score was tied.

"Time out! Time out!" Coach Blue shouted out to the referee.

Ice Cream walked slowly back to his bench.

"What's wrong, Cream? How you feel?" Coach Blue asked.

"I feel okay, Coach," he answered.

"Okay, man. Let's bring it home," Coach Blue demanded.

"Okay, Coach." Ice Cream was slow to speak.

"Ice Cream is looking a little weak in the face," Fats voiced out to Coach Blue.

"I noticed myself, Fats," Coach Blue responded.

The game horn sounded off to start and finish up this championship title. Ice Cream, again, was walking slowly back to his free throw line. The south team shooter could tell that something was wrong, with Ice Cream walking slowly.

"I have a feeling Cream will miss some of his free throw shots in these last three minutes." Coach Blue looked back at his teammates.

Fats, Range, and Deep stood up the whole time, hoping for a victory. At the one-minute mark, the game was still tied. Ice Cream, so far, was hanging in there with the south team shooter. With forty-five seconds left, the fans stood up, cheering and wondering who would win this championship game. The north and west teams were also watching from their previous game in their seats. With three seconds left, the game was still tied.

"Oh no!" Coach Blue and the boys shouted out.

Ice Cream missed his last free throw shot at the buzzer, but the south team shooter made his shot, and so the south team won the championship tournament title. The south team and their fans were rejoicing in their victory.

"That's okay, Ice Cream. You will make a winning free throw shot at another game later on in the future," Coach Blue declared.

"Thanks, Coach," he responded.

"Hey, man, you did great. Another time will come." Fats, Range, and Deep gathered around him, hugging one another.

"Hey, Ice Cream, it is okay," the girls encouraged him.

The sports reporters were still interviewing the fantastic four and Coach Blue regardless of their loss.

"I told you boys we was going to win!" The south team shooters blurted out negative remarks to the dream boys.

"Come on, Cream. Let's go." Good Pass grabbed his hand and started walking toward the locker room.

"We coming too," the rest of his teammates and their girlfriends also mentioned.

All the east team parents plus Coach Blue's wife and the girls were waiting outside the locker room.

The crew began cheering when the fantastic four and Coach Blue approached the hallway. "Go, East! Go, East! Go, East!"

The sports reporters followed them all the way back to the bus, still interviewing the boys and Coach Blue.

"Thank you, guys." Coach Blue waved to the sports reporters. "Hey, everyone, let's stop by a restaurant to eat something," Coach Blue voiced out.

"Sounds great!" they all responded to Coach Blue.

When they all arrived at the restaurant and walked in, the customers greeted them by clapping and cheering for them.

"We saw the tournament. Sorry about the loss," some of the customers voiced out to them.

"That's okay," Coach Blue responded.

While they were all eating, it was silent for a few minutes.

"Hey, Ice Cream, do not worry about that last free throw shot. You will make it the next time around." Coach Blue noticed his expression.

"Honey, let him go through his moments," Coach Blue's wife verbalized.

"Okay, dear. You are right," Coach Blue responded.

The girls and rebounders as well as the parents were supporting them.

"Okay, is everybody finished eating? The time is getting late," Coach Blue voiced out.

They all began cleaning up their tables.

"Good luck next time!" some the customers voiced out to them.

"Okay, thank you." The whole crew waved back to the customers, approaching the exit door.

"Hey, guys, we have to get ready for the summer camp next week," Coach Blue announced to his dream boys. "Then you guys can head back to Virginia."

When they arrived back at the hotel, they all rested in the main lobby for a few minutes. The north, south, and west teams had already packed up and left the hotel.

"Listen up, guys," Coach Blue voiced out. "While we are here, let's discuss the summer camp."

"Okay, Coach Blue," the boys responded.

"We are going to bed," the parents and the girls stated.

The cheerleaders and rebounders left as well.

"You guys will be very important in this training camp," Coach Blue declared. "Just have your free throw game ready to teach younger kids, fellows."

"Yes, sir, Coach. We will be ready," the boys responded.

"It is 10:00 p.m., guys. Go to your room and get some sleep."

"Okay, Coach Blue," the dream boys responded. "Good night, Coach."

"Good night, guys," Coach Blue and his wife responded.

The fantastic four arrived at their room and sat on their beds for a minute.

"Hey, man, I am sorry for missing that last free throw shot," Ice Cream mumbled.

"We are not upset with you, Cream!" Fats shouted out loud.

"You will make up that missed free throw someday," Range voiced out to Ice Cream.

"Yeah, we got your back, Ice Cream," Deep stated.

"Let's get some sleep and be ready for the summer camp," Fats declared.

While the boys were sleeping, Ice Cream could not sleep right away, thinking about that missed free throw shot at the championship game. Early that Sunday morning, he woke up on his bed still thinking about that missed shot. The other boys were still asleep at 7:00 a.m. Ice Cream rose up from his bed and made himself a paper ball, beginning to shoot it in the trash can like a free throw shot. He was determined to make up for that missed free throw in some game one day. At the same time, he reflected on the first grade, shooting in the trash can. He practiced for thirty minutes.

Fats overheard this knocking noise from the trash can. "Hey, man, you are working out early." He rose up out of his bed quickly. "I am going to shoot too," he voiced out.

"What's going on?" Range and Deep rolled over and saw the action going on. "We coming to shoot also." They rushed forward quickly.

At 9:00 a.m., Ice Cream noticed the sports reporters on their television talking about the championship game last Saturday night. "Hey, man, look," Ice Cream voiced out to his teammates. "They are showing some highlights of the championship game."

"Oh man, they showing you, Cream, missing your last free throw shot," Deep stated.

"I will stay focused next time if I have to shoot another winning free throw shot for sure," Ice Cream declared to his teammates.

"Hey, guys, it is 9:30 a.m. Let's eat some breakfast," Fats said.

"I will call the girls' room. Maybe they will join us also," Ice Cream voiced out. "Good morning, Good Pass," Ice Cream communicated to her on the phone.

"Good morning, Ice Cream," she answered.

"Me and the guys headed for breakfast. You girls coming?" he asked.

"Sure, Ice Cream. We will be there," she responded. "Meet us in the hallway at 10:20 a.m."

"Okay, great," Ice Cream answered. "Hey, man, the girls are coming too. Be ready at 10:20 a.m., fellows," he stated to his teammates.

"Let's get dressed right away," Fats voiced out.

The fantastic four were ready to leave their room at 10:18 a.m. They arrived at the girls' door, waiting for them to come out at 10:20 a.m. exactly.

"Good morning, fellows." The girls approached them outside their room door.

"Good morning," the dream boys responded.

The parents were already downstairs eating their breakfast earlier. The dreams boys and the girls headed to meet with the parents to eat. When they arrived, there were a lot of people eating as well. The people started to cheer and clap for the east team, showing support and encouragement to them.

"Hey, man, this is nice," Deep and Range voiced out.

"Yeah, man, it is," Fats and Ice Cream voiced out as well.

"Wow!" The girls showed excitement.

They were all eating their breakfast and talking about the previous championship game plus the summer camp starting next week.

Chapter 9

THE SUMMER FREE THROW CAMP

Everybody was present now at the breakfast lobby, waiting on Coach Blue and his wife to set up a meeting for the summer camp.

"Hey, Ice Cream, I am tired," Good Pass voiced out.

"Okay, let's walk into the main lobby to rest," Ice Cream responded.

The parents and the rest of the crew followed them to rest as well.

"Hey, man, I am ready for the summer camp to train kids younger than we are on free throws," Ice Cream announced to his teammates.

Five minutes later, the hotel phone was ringing at the front desk.

"Excuse me. Is there someone named Ice Cream here?" the desk clerk asked the crew.

"Yes, that's me," Ice Cream responded.

"Your coach wants you on the phone," she replied.

Ice Cream rushed out of his chair to receive the phone from the clerk. "Thank you," Ice Cream stated.

"You are welcome," she responded.

"Hello, Coach Blue," he answered.

"Hi, Cream," Coach Blue answered. "Let everyone know my wife and I will be there to talk about the summer camp, and the rebounders will be there also."

"Okay, Coach Blue," Ice Cream replied. Ice Cream slammed the phone down, running toward the crew with a happy smile. "Hey, everybody, Coach Blue said he will be here at 1:00 p.m. to have a summer camp meeting."

"Great! We get to train kids our own age," Fats blurted out.

"That's cool," Deep and Range voiced out as well.

At 1:00 p.m., Coach Blue and his wife arrived at the hotel.

"Good afternoon, everyone," Coach Blue and his wife articulated.

"Good afternoon," the crew responded.

"Okay, everybody, let's head to the conference room for our meeting about the summer camp," Coach Blue stated. "First of all, thank you all for showing up, and I see my rebounders are here too. Great!" Coach Blue looked on very proudly. "My guys, it is very important to train these kids how to shoot free throws to develop their percentage in the future."

"Yes, sir, Coach!" the fantastic four reacted.

"Rebounders, make sure your passes are sharp and straight to the shooters," Coach Blue ordered.

"Yes, sir, Coach!" the rebounders responded.

"On Monday morning, seven o'clock, I will pick up everybody here with the bus to arrive at the camp," Coach Blue declared. "The meeting is over. Everyone have a good day and be safe."

"You too, Coach Blue and Mrs. Blue," the crew responded.

"Thank you," Coach Blue and Mrs. Blue responded.

They all exited the conference room.

"Hey, boys and girls, let's eat an early dinner so we can get back to our rooms to be ready in the morning," the parents stated.

"Okay," the dream boys and the girls answered.

The rebounders checked into their rooms to be in place for the camp in the morning at seven o'clock. After they all ate dinner, it was time to depart for the night.

"Okay, boys and girls, get to your rooms and sleep. We have to get up at 5:00 a.m.," the parents ordered.

When the dream boys entered their room, they sat on their beds, watching television.

"Hey, man, let's shoot some paper balls in the trash can for a short practice," Range stated.

"Sounds good, man," Ice Cream replied.

"You need it, man," Deep voiced.

"Be nice, Deep," Ice Cream blurted out.

"Come on, fellows, let's do this," Fats and Range voiced out.

After the fantastic four worked out their paper ball practice, they exited to bed. Early Monday morning, the dream boys rose up at five o'clock sharp.

"Hey, Ice Cream, camp day!" Deep shouted out.

"Yeah, man!" Ice Cream, Fats, and Range responded.

The parents and girls plus the rebounders were up as well. At 6:00 a.m., they all met at the breakfast lobby to eat a small meal. Around 6:50 a.m., they were all finished and ready to meet Coach Blue and his wife plus the rebounders in the main lobby at 7:00 a.m.

"Hey, look, look. It is Coach Blue and his wife coming in," Fats blurted out.

"Good morning, everyone. I see you all are ready and healthy," Coach Blue and his wife stated.

"Okay, let's head for the bus," Coach Blue ordered.

The camp began at 9:00 a.m.

"Listen up, my dream boys and rebounders! We have to do very well at this camp all week long with great conductivity," Coach Blue mentioned.

"Yes, sir, Coach Blue!" the dream boys and rebounders responded.

As they were all riding to USC, the dream boys were very focused and ready to teach free throws. When they approached the camp, they took notice that there were a lot of people out there.

"Wow! Look, Cream. Look at all those people walking inside," Fats blurted out on the bus.

The bus driver headed around the back of the university to drop off the crew. At 8:00 a.m., Coach Blue and his fantastic four were inside their locker room, and the rebounders exited to the court in their places under the basket.

"Hey, Coach, you and your team have five minutes to start the summer camp," the camp athletic director instructed.

"Okay, thank you," Coach Blue responded. "Okay, fellows, let's put on a good show and train these kids well."

"Sure, Coach!" the fantastic four reacted.

"Get your basketballs and let's head out to the court with your rebounders," Coach Blue declared.

As they left the locker room, the dream boys were looking very serious.

"Wow, man! There are a lot of people here," Range voiced out.

"I know, man," Ice Cream responded.

"Come on, man, stay focused," Fats and Deep said back to their teammates.

The four boys arrived center court to a stop, looking around the arena at the crowd. The camp athletic director approached Coach Blue with a microphone in his hand plus information on the camp.

"Good morning, everybody. All of this week, Coach Blue and his team will show some nice dynamic free throw shooting skills and train our kids how to shoot very well because free throws help win ball games and are very important. Thank you. Let's give them a hand!" the director verbalized clearly to the fans. "Okay, Coach, it's your world." The camp director gave him the microphone.

Coach Blue introduced his team, the rebounders, and the crew. "First, my guys will shoot free throws at each basket to show you young kids and fans how the free throws are properly shot from the line. They will shoot fifty free throws each, and our rebounders will throw great bounce and chest passes to them. Okay, boys, you can start shooting now," Coach Blue ordered.

While the fantastic four were shooting, the fans were very impressed to see each of them shoot 95 percent of those free throws. The sports reporters were tuning in, and the parents and girls plus Coach Blue's wife were very proud of what they saw as well.

"Way to go, fellows!" the girls shouted out to their dream boys.

Fifteen minutes had gone by, and the free throw shooting show was coming to an end.

"Let's give them a hand!" Coach Blue addressed the fans. "Now it is time for our training session. The boys will train the kids, starting with free throw dynamic drills and then level one through five free throw shooting drills," he explained to the fans. "After those drills, they will train them on free throw dynamics with rhythm drills, and the camp will be over for today."

There were forty kids aged seven to thirteen, all boys. For the younger boys, aged seven to nine, the camp director lowered the basket to seven feet. The dream boys were doing very well explaining and showing all the free throw skills and drills to the kids. Coach Blue was rotating from each basket with the microphone, explaining to the fans what each drill was about.

At noon, Coach Blue closed out the camp for that Monday. "You guys did great training these young kids."

"Thank you, Coach Blue," the fantastic four responded.

"Hey, Coach Blue, the sports reporters want to interview you and us," Ice Cream voiced out.

"Sure," Coach Blue responded.

"I'll start off with you, Coach Blue," one of the sports reporters asked. "How long have you been coaching these four great free throw shooters on your team?"

"Well, I met these wonderful young teens in Virginia at the ice cream store around one year ago," Coach Blue responded.

"Wow!" the sports reporter replied. "I believe these young men on your team will be great professional free throw shooters one day."

"Yes, they told me when I first met them, and I am looking forward to seeing that happen for them boys," Coach Blue responded.

"Okay, thank you, Coach Blue, for your time. Can I talk to your shooters?" the sports reporter asked.

"Sure," Coach Blue answered.

The sports reporter walked over to Ice Cream and his teammates. "Hello, young men. My name is Randy. I am with LA Sports."

"Hello, sir," the dream boys answered.

"Your coach pointed me to you guys," the sports reporter verbalized. "How long have you guys been shooting free throws and training great like this?"

"We have been shooting free throws since the first grade, and we just started to teach this year," Ice Cream voiced out.

"That's wonderful, guys," Randy stated.

"Thank you, sir," the dream boys answered.

"We will be tuning in all week here at the camp," Randy stated.

"Okay, sir," the boys responded. "Hey, Coach Blue, we finished the interview with Mr. Randy."

"Okay, great, guys. You all did well today. Let's continue this all week long," Coach Blue voiced out.

"Yes, sir, Coach!" the dream boys responded.

Every day at the camp, the dream boys did supernaturally great training those young kids on their free throws. The kids increased from 60 percent to 90 percent at the free throw line by the last day. On that Friday morning at the camp, the dream boys felt that they had done a good job to help the kids. Word had gotten out all week to the city manager about the fantastic four shooting and training these younger kids at the camp. During that Friday at the camp, the city manager made a special trip out there to see for himself. He was amazed at how the dream boys could shoot free throws like that at a young age. The final hour of the summer camp had arrived to close out the whole week.

Coach Blue closed out the camp with his remarks. "Thank you all for allowing us to come out here to show our free throw skills and train your kids to be good free throw shooters. Also, I thank the camp director too and the city manager for coming plus the fans for your support all week long."

All the fans started cheering and clapping while the dream boys and Coach Blue bowed down and, waving, headed to the locker room.

The city manager and the camp director addressed Coach Blue in the locker room. "Thank you, Coach, for what your dream boys have done for our community, training our young kids to shoot free throws."

"You are welcome. I am glad we can be of great service to your kids and their families," Coach Blue responded.

The city manager and camp director left with great smiles on their faces.

"Great job, fellows. Let's get dressed and meet the crew in the hallway," Coach Blue ordered.

When they arrived out in the hallway, the sports reporters were also there for the last remarks from Coach Blue. The crew started cheering and clapping.

"Thank you." Coach Blue waved to everybody.

"Tell me, Coach Blue, what is next on your agenda for your dream boys?" one of the sports reporters asked.

"Well, we are headed back to the hotel to get the boys and girls and the parents ready to fly back to Virginia early Saturday morning," Coach Blue stated.

"Okay. We will come to Virginia and tune in on your fantastic four shooting their free throws at their high school basketball games," the sports reporter responded.

"Sounds great," Coach Blue responded.

The sports reporters closed out their last interview. "Have a safe trip back to the hotel, and for the boys and the rest, have a safe trip back to Virginia!"

The crew, riding on the bus, headed back to the hotel.

"Hey, everyone, the hotel staff left word with my wife that they fixed a great going-back-home dinner in the breakfast lobby," Coach Blue stated.

"Oh, cool!" the dream boys and the girls responded.

"Very nice," the parents voiced out.

They arrived at the lobby.

"Wow! This is nice, man!" Ice Cream turned and look at his teammates.

"Let's eat. I'm hungry," Fats blurted out.

"Me too," Range and Deep mentioned as well.

The parents addressed their kids. "Go to the restroom and wash your hands."

"We all will spend the night here and see you guys off to the airport on Saturday morning," Coach Blue stated.

"Okay, sounds great. Thank you," the parents responded.

After the special dinner that the hotel staff had provided for them, it was time for them to exit to their rooms for an early takeoff on Saturday morning. After the dream boys arrived at their room, they started packing up their things. Before they went to bed, the boys did it one more time, shooting paper balls into the trash can, to close out their two weeks in LA.

Chapter 10

FLIGHT BACK HOME

"Hey, fellows, it's time to get up. It is 6:00 a.m.," Ice Cream voiced out to his teammates.

"Ten more minutes, man," Deep voiced.

"Come on, Cream. Let us sleep in a little longer," Fats and Range announced.

"No, guys. We have to eat and finish packing, man," Ice Cream stated.

"Okay, man." Fats, Range, and Deep slowly rose out of their beds.

Ice Cream came out with "I will call Mama to see what time we will eat."

"Okay, man," his teammates answered.

"Hey, guys, Mama said we will meet at 8:00 a.m. downstairs in the lobby," Ice Cream declared.

"Okay, we are getting dressed," his teammates responded.

At 8:00 a.m., the entire crew met to eat.

"Good morning, everyone," Coach Blue and his wife voiced out.

"Good morning," they all answered.

Coach Blue stood up about ten minutes later to make an announcement. "Thank you all for coming to LA. Boys, you guys have done wonderful in the tournament and the summer camp. Let's all finish up our food and head on the bus. Your plane leaves at 11:15 a.m."

"Okay, Coach Blue," they all answered to him.

After they ate, they all went back to their rooms to get their things to load up on the bus.

"Everybody ready to ride?" Coach Blue voiced out.

"Yes!" they all answered.

While riding to the LA airport, the dream boys and the girls were sleeping. The parents, cheerleaders, and rebounders were in and out themselves.

"We are here," Coach Blue voiced out.

As they all started walking through the airport and headed to their gate, they all hugged one another to say their goodbyes. Coach Blue and his wife plus the rebounders and cheerleaders were looking out the big window, watching the plane take off.

"Okay, everybody, let's head back to the hotel," Coach Blue voiced out. "Ice Cream's parents will let me know when they arrive in Virginia."

The remaining people back at the hotel departed and went home. Late that evening, around seven o'clock, Coach Blue's home phone was ringing.

"Hey, honey, get the phone!" Coach Blue voiced out to his wife.

"Hey, honey, it is Ice Cream's parents! They landed safely!" she voiced out to her husband.

"Okay, great! Tell them I will come to see the boys play one high school game!" Coach Blue responded.

"Tell Coach Blue that sounds great," Ice Cream's parents replied to his wife on the phone.

On that Sunday evening, the fantastic four and the girls headed to the ice cream store to eat ice cream cones.

"Hey, everybody, this brings back memories," Ice Cream voiced out.

"Yeah, man!" his teammates and the girls responded.

The girls noticed something. "Hey, look over there. It's a trash can."

"Let's shoot with our napkins like we did back in the day," Fats and Range mentioned.

The boys started to shoot their paper napkins into the trash can fifteen feet away from their table. The customers noticed the dream boys and began to cheer out while they were making the shots.

"Excuse us, young man. We saw you guys on television in LA shooting at the tournament." "Thanks," the dream boys responded.

"You boys can shoot those free throws very good," two customers mentioned.

"We are going outside to the court and shooting real free throws in a minute," Ice Cream said.

"Okay, we might come out there to see you guys shoot," the two customers stated.

"Okay, sounds great," Ice Cream voiced out.

When the dream boys and the girls left to go to the court, a few more customers followed them.

"Wow, you guys can really shoot those free throws like in the tournament!" the customers blurted out.

After a while, the court was getting packed, with more people coming from all angles to see these free throws. After the fantastic four finished their work out on the court, the customers were very pleased by how they could shoot free throws.

"Hey, young fellows, it will be time for you guys to start high school basketball, right?" the customers asked.

"Yes, we are ready," the dream boys responded.

"Okay, we will be there at your games to see you shoot free throws at the line. Goodbye and have a nice day!" The customers left the court, waving.

"Goodbye!" the dream boys responded.

"Hey, everybody, it is late, and we have to get ready for high school coming in three weeks," Range stated.

"That's right, man," Ice Cream voiced out. "Hey, fellows, let's go home now."

"We will call one another to go school shopping together," Block mentioned to the crew.

"Okay, let's leave," Set Shot stated.

They all left the court and departed for their homes to get ready for high school.

Chapter 11

GETTING READY FOR HIGH SCHOOL

When September came around, it was time for the dream boys and the girls to attend high school. The day before school started, the crew met at the court near the ice cream store.

"Hey, man, have you guys been school shopping yet?" Ice Cream mentioned to his teammates.

"Yes, sir. Man, we all did that already," Deep answered.

"Okay, okay," Ice Cream responded.

"We have our clothes too already," Dunk declared as well for the girls.

"Okay, girls," Range responded.

"Let's get this short free throw workout done. I have to get back home early for school," Fats blurted out to everybody.

After the dream boys finished their free throw practice, they all departed and went home to prepare for school the next day.

"Good morning, everybody," Ice Cream articulated at the bus stop.

"Good morning, Ice Cream," his teammates and the girls as well as the other students at the bus stop responded.

"There are a lot of students out here," Set Shot mumbled softly.

"I see Set Shot," Block responded.

"This bus will be crowded," Dunk stated.

When the bus arrived, the fantastic four and the girls stepped on board the bus.

Everybody started clapping and cheering for them. "Go, East! Go, East! Go, East!"

"Thank you, thank you," the four stars responded.

While riding to high school, the students were telling the four stars about how they couldn't wait to see those free throws during basketball season. When the dream boys and the girls arrived at school, the boys had so much attention about their great free throw shooting skills, the girls had to keep them focused on their schoolwork. Every day the students were talking about the dream boys and how hopefully, they could help get Swish High School to the state championship making free throws. Last year, Swish High School lost a lot of games at the free throw line. After school was over on the first day, the fantastic four wanted to meet the head coach.

"Hey, Ice Cream, let's go to the coach's office to find out about tryouts for the basketball team," Fats voiced out.

"Great idea, Fats!" Range and Deep responded.

"Okay, man, let's go," Ice Cream responded as well.

"Hey, where you guys going?" Good Pass asked.

"We are going to find the head basketball coach," Ice Cream answered.

"Can we go?"

"Sure, girls. Come on," Deep answered.

They all left the main hallway and headed to the basketball office. *Knock! Knock!* Ice Cream gently knocked on the basketball office door.

"Hello, boys and girls. I know you guys. You are the four great free throw shooters. My name is Coach Wilson. I am the head basketball coach here at Swish High School. I will be the basketball coach until you guys graduate," Coach Wilson declared. "I saw the free throw tournament. It was amazing."

"Thank you, Coach Wilson," the dream boys responded.

"I am excited to have you guys here to play for my team for all four years," he stated.

"Thank you, Coach Wilson," the boys reacted again.

"Who are these four young ladies?" Coach Wilson asked.

"They are our friends. We have been friends since the first grade," Ice Cream answered.

"That's wonderful!" Coach Wilson responded. "I assume you boys are here to find out when basketball starts."

"Yes, sir, Coach Wilson!" The fantastic four were steamed up ready.

"It will begin in November. If you boys want to work out in the gym, I have an hour left before I go home," Coach Wilson stated.

"Okay. Thank you, Coach Wilson." The boys were juiced up and ready to go.

"Let's head to the gym. I want to see you guys shoot free throws."

Coach Wilson accelerated to the gym with the crew behind him. While they were going to the gym, Coach Wilson was mentioning to the dream boys last year why his team had not made it to the state tournament.

"Hey, guys, we did terrible at the free throw line last year," Coach Wilson stated.

"How did that happen, Coach?" Ice Cream asked.

"Well, son, I think my team last year did not take their free throws seriously. We lost a lot of games from missing free throws," Coach Wilson voiced out to the crew.

"Wow!" Fats blurted out.

"I know this year and the next three years, we will have a good chance to make the state tournament," Coach Wilson stated.

"Why?" Range asked.

"You four guys are here," Coach Wilson voiced out to them.

"Well, thank you, Coach Wilson. We will do the best we can at the line," Range responded.

"Coach, I know these boys. They can shoot free throws real good," Set Shot voiced out.

They arrived at the gym, and the fantastic four rushed to the free throw line, ready to shoot.

"Wow, guys, you are at least 97 percent! That is amazing. I am very impressed." Coach Wilson was fired up from what he saw from the dream boys. "I want to win a state title for the first time in this school's history," he stated to the girls sitting on the bleachers while they were watching the boys shoot.

"Hopefully, Coach Wilson, the boys will help out to win the state," Block voiced out.

"I believe we will, girls," Coach Wilson responded.

When basketball season came around, Coach Wilson won a lot of games from the free throw line. During the last game of the regular season tournament, Coach Wilson's team had to win to qualify for the state tournament. During that last game, the score was tied at sixty-two points. Coach Wilson's team had the ball with seven seconds left in the fourth quarter. Fats passed the ball to Ice Cream, and he drove to the basket and create a foul. Ice Cream had to shoot a one-and-one free throw shot.

"Ice Cream, make these free throws," Fats mumbled to him before he shot his free throws.

Everybody in the gym stood up to see whether Ice Cream would make his first free throw shot. *Swish.* The ball went into the basket, and the home team students went crazy. *Swish* again! The second free throw went into the basket. When the other team received the ball again, there was not enough time for them to score. The game horn sounded off, so Swish High School won many games and advanced to the first round of the state championship next Friday night.

"Yes, sir, we made it!" Coach Wilson shouted out with joy around his team and students on the court.

"Yes, sir, Ice Cream! Nice free throws!" Fats, Range, and Deep, overjoyed all around, were also giving high fives and hugs. The girls and parents were rejoicing too.

"Hey, guys, let's head to the locker room and get dressed," Coach Wilson ordered. "Good game, fellows! Hurry up, guys. Let's get out of here quickly to get ready for next week's state championship game."

"Yes, sir, Coach!" The dream boys were elated.

On Monday morning, back at Swish High School, the week of the state championship game began, and the school had a pep rally.

"Thank you, students, parents, family, and school staff, for supporting our team all season," Coach Wilson stated at the pep rally. "My team did a great job this year advancing to the state championship coming up on Friday night at the coliseum."

After the pep rally was over, they all exited back to class, and the families went back home. The local news sports reporters and the LA sports reporters started interviewing the fantastic four and Coach Wilson.

"On Friday night, what kind of game plan will you guys bring to the championship?" the sports reporters asked the dream boys.

"We will be ready to win and make our free throws," Ice Cream answered.

"Okay, fellows," the reporters responded.

"Yes, sir! We will be ready to shoot our best."

"Yes, sir!" Fats, Range, and Deep supported Ice Cream's comment.

Everyone at the school and all the family members were very excited about the state game. Coach Wilson let his team practice every day but Friday.

"Hey, guys, listen up!" Coach Wilson declared. "Tomorrow we will report to the team meeting room at 6:45 p.m. before the state game."

"Okay, Coach Wilson," his team answered.

"Also, guys, we will head to the locker room after the meeting for the game," Coach Wilson declared.

"Yes, sir, Coach!" the team responded again.

The next day, on that Friday evening, right at six forty-five, Coach Wilson and his team reported to the meeting room.

"Okay, guys, listen up. Please, *please* stay focused on your free throws. Keep your body still and your follow-through hand straight plus your feet square to the basket," Coach Wilson verbalized.

"Yes, sir, Coach!" they responded.

"Okay, now let's get into our uniforms for the state game," Coach Wilson stated.

The team started to dress up for the game.

"Hey, man, that's my number," Fats said to Range.

"Oh! My fault, man," Range responded.

"Hey, fellows, hurry up. The time is getting close," Ice Cream fired out to his teammates.

"Yeah, man, we have to win this game tonight," Deep voiced out.

"Everybody ready? Let's join hands and pray."

Coach Wilson headed back into the locker room to check on his team. After the prayer, they all exited to the court to warm up. The coliseum was packed from top to bottom.

"Wow! There's a lot of people in here," Range voiced out.

"Hey, Range, stay focused like Coach Wilson said," Ice Cream declared.

"You right, Cream," Range responded.

At 7:30 p.m., both teams were warming up. All the family members and friends plus all the Swish High School students and staff were sitting behind Coach Wilson's team bench. The fans were making a lot of cheering noise for their teams. The game horn sounded off; both teams rushed to their benches.

"Okay, guys, this is it. Let's get out there and win this game for our school," Coach Wilson voiced out in the team huddle.

"Yes, sir, man! Let's win!" Ice Cream was steamed up with his teammates.

Both teams entered the court to start playing. The first half of the game was very close. Coach Wilson's team was only down two points. The dream boys were in the starting lineup for Coach Wilson's team. The dream boys were making their free throws with no problem. They were shooting 100 percent each from the free throw line. The local sports reporters and the LA reporters were amazed by how the dream boys were making those free throws in a row plus shooting from outside, playing defense. At halftime, the fans were talking to one another about how well the dream boys could shoot free throws. Plus, the fans were amazed at how great future drum artist Dion Langley and his crew could play those drums at the halftime show.

Coach Wilson discussed with his team the second half. "Hey, guys, let me go out to the court and check on the time left on the clock to start the second half."

"Okay, Coach," his team responded.

"Wow, you guys! Those young men out there are playing those drums like pros at the half," Coach Wilson mentioned to his team back in the locker room. "Okay, fellows, back to work. We have one minute to head out. Let's put it in on three."

"Free throws! Free throws! Free throws! Let's go!"

They approached the court to warm up for the second half. The game horn sounded off to start the second half. The dream boys were still making their free throws like butter. The girls sitting behind them were also very proud of their boyfriends making their free throws. As the third quarter went by onto the fourth quarter, the game was now tied, sixty-five to sixty-five. With thirty-five seconds left to play for the state title, everybody began to stand up. With twenty-five seconds left to play, Ice Cream was fouled by the other team player. He had to shoot two free throws and made both of them.

"Yes, sir, Ice Cream!" his teammates shouted from the bench.

The fans for Swish High School went crazy and were cheering very loudly for their team. Coach Wilson's team was now leading by two points with twenty seconds left for the title.

"Defense! Defense!" Coach Wilson shouted out loud to his team on the court. "Oh no, Fats! Don't foul! My goodness, Fats, why?" Coach Wilson stomped the floor with anger as his face dropped to sadness.

The other team player had to shoot two free throws, and both shots counted as two points.

"Oh man!" Deep shouted out.

The score was tied again, sixty-seven to sixty-seven, with twelve seconds left to play. Ice Cream was coming up the court with the basketball in full speed, looking to create a move.

"Okay, Ice Cream, let's get it! Let's get it!" Coach Wilson voiced out to him.

Ice Cream drove very hard to the basket and was fouled by the other team player with five seconds left to play.

"Let's do it, Cream!" Good Pass and the girls were jumping up and down with all the school fans and family members, knowing he would make his free throws.

"Make this, Cream!" Fats, Range, Deep, and his other teammates high-fived Ice Cream at the free throw line.

As Ice Cream approached the free throw line, he looked very relaxed and ready.

"I know my man will make these free throws. He has been shooting like this since we were kids," Good Pass joyfully mentioned to people around her at her seat.

Before the official gave Ice Cream the basketball to shoot, the other team members on the court were making negative remarks to him to make him lose concentration when he started to shoot his free throws. When Ice Cream received the basketball from the official, he came to a pause. He looked to his left at Good Pass with a smile, and she blew a kiss at him. He went back to focus and took one bounce. *Swish!* The ball went into the basket. After Ice Cream made his first shot, everybody went crazy, shouting and cheering all over the arena. It took at least three minutes to calm everybody down so he could shoot his second free throw shot.

"Yes, sir, Cream!" Fats, Range, Deep, and the other teammates voiced out loud.

"One more, Cream! Swish again!"

Everybody started cheering again but not that long with two seconds left to play for the state title. The other team rushed back down their end of the court to score, but time had run out, and the game was over. All the fans, students, and family members rushed down to the court, congratulating the team. The girls rushed to the dream boys, hugging and cheering for them. The sports reporters started interviewing Coach Wilson and the boys' former free throw coach, LA visitor Coach Blue, with a sixty-nine-to-sixty-seven victory. This was the first time Swish High School won a state championship title.

After the celebrating, it was time to give out the rewards. The game anchorman announced that he had never seen a great game like this before shooting free throws. Also, Coach Wilson made a great speech on how his team had played so well all season. Ice Cream received the MVP free throw award for the year. Also, Coach Wilson acknowledged the dream boys on how well they had shot free throws to help win a lot of games this year. Coach Blue also announced how well the dream boys had been shooting good free throws since he met them at the ice cream store.

"Yeah, man, we did it!" Deep voiced out to his teammates.

"Yes, sir, Deep!" Ice Cream and the rest responded.

After everything was said and done, the team exited back to the locker room to change. The girls and family members as well as some students were waiting for the team to come out into the hallway. Coach Blue and his wife plus the LA sports reporters exited back out west to go home. When the dream boys exited into the hallway, everybody started clapping and cheering again to congratulate the boys. Ice Cream was holding up the team trophy, happy with good spirit. The time was around 11:00 p.m., and they all said good night to one another, walking to their vehicles.

"Hey, man, let's call one another in the morning," Ice Cream stated to his free throw buddies.

Then they left to go home for the night.

"Hey, good morning, Good Pass." Ice Cream called her right at eleven o'clock that Saturday morning.

"Good morning, Cream," she answered. "Nice game and good free throw shooting last night."

"Thank you," Ice Cream responded.

"Good morning, Block." Fats called her.

"Good morning, Fats," Block answered. "You guys were great at the line last night."

"Thank you, Block," Fats responded.

"Good morning, Dunk." Range called her.

"Good morning, Range," Dunk answered. "You guys were good at the line last night."

"Thank you," Range responded.

"Good morning, Set Shot." Deep called her.

"Good morning, Deep," Set Shot answered. "You guys had a great game and were super at the line last night."

"Thank you, Set Shot," Deep answered.

Early that same morning, the parents collected their newspapers and saw articles and pictures of the state game. All the family members and friends were calling one another, talking about the state game. Later on that evening, the parents arranged a celebration dinner for the dream boys at a local restaurant. When they all arrived at the restaurant, the customers rushed over to the dream boys, congratulating them. They admittedly began taking pictures and getting autographs from the dream boys. When the parents purchased everybody food, the manager paid for the meals for the boys winning the state title.

"Okay, everybody, it's getting late," the parents stated.

"Ice Cream, you have to throw the rest of your food away, son," Ice Cream's parents uttered.

"Okay," he answered.

The crew were packing up, ready to leave the restaurant.

"Thank you, Manager, for treating us," the parents voiced out.

"You are welcome. It was nice talking to you guys," the manager voiced out.

"Hopefully, next season, we will win the state again," Fats voiced out.

"Sounds good," the manager responded.

They all went back to Ice Cream's house and went their separate ways back home. When Sunday morning arrived, the dream boys rested all day until late that evening. The girls were thinking about calling the dream boys at around four o'clock that evening.

"Hey, Block, what are you doing?" Good Pass called her.

"Nothing, girl," Block answered.

"Okay. I was thinking about contacting the boys about going to the ice cream store at 5:30 p.m."

"Okay, Good Pass. That sounds great," Block answered.

"Okay, I will call Dunk."

"Okay, I will call Set Shot."

All the girls agreed to call the boys. The dream boys agreed to go to the ice cream store at 5:30 p.m. They all met at Ice Cream's house, but it was raining outside.

"Hey, guys, we will drive you all to the ice cream store and let you stay there for thirty minutes," the parents voiced out.

"Wow! Okay, sounds great," the dream boys and the girls replied.

They all arrived at the ice cream store.

"Okay, guys, we will be back in thirty minutes," the parents declared.

The customers begin to clap and cheer for the dream boys for winning the state game.

"Thank you, thank you," the dream boys responded.

The young crew sat down to eat their ice cream cones.

"Hey, man, look over there—the trash can," Deep blurted out loud.

"Hey, guys, are you thinking what I'm thinking?" Fats voiced out.

"Yes, sir! Let's shoot!" Ice Cream blurted out.

The dream boys began to shoot their paper balls in the trash can like back in the day. Everybody in the ice cream store stopped suddenly and watched the dream boys shoot paper balls in the trash can. The girls were smiling and proud of their boyfriends making those shots. By that time, the parents arrived back at the ice cream store.

"Hey, look at those boys. They are shooting paper balls again," Ice Cream's parents voiced out to the other parents.

"Yes, indeed," the other parents responded.

"I see your sons making those shots in the can like it's nothing," the store manager voiced out to the parents.

"Yes, they've loved to shoot them like free throws since the first grade," the parents replied. "Okay, boys and girls, it's time to head back home. Pack it up."

"Okay," the dream boys and the girls answered.

They all began to leave, heading to Ice Cream's house. The parents ordered pizza and soft drinks for everyone.

"Hey, look! Look what's on TV!" Range shouted out. "They are showing highlights of the state game!" Range was steamed up with joy.

"Oh man! Yes, sir!" Ice Cream voiced out.

"Wow!" The girls spoke out.

"Go, boys!" Deep's parents voiced out.

"That was a nice game," Set Shot's parents mentioned.

"You guys shot your free throws well," Block's parents stated.

"Thank you, thank you," the dream boys responded.

Everybody was very happy about the highlights on television.

"Well, it is getting late. Let's pack it up, everybody," Ice Cream's parents declared.

"That's right—school tomorrow," Dunk's parents mentioned.

"Oh man, I can't wait to see the school students react to us," Fats voiced out.

"That's right, Fats. We won the state championship game, man!" Ice Cream stated.

On Monday, when the dream boys and the girls arrived at school, all the students and staff workers began to congratulate the dream boys. Every time the dream boys entered their classes, the students began to clap and cheer to them, along with Coach Wilson. During their classes, most of the conversations were about the state championship game. That Friday, Coach Wilson planned for everyone in the whole school to report to the gym by 1:00 p.m.

"Listen up, everyone!" Coach Wilson declared. "Our principal, Mr. Jumper, has something to say."

"Good afternoon, everyone," Principal Jumper modulated. "We have a presentation gift for our state champs. Come on in, champs!"

Principal Jumper invited the basketball team into the gym center court. When the team and Coach Wilson arrived, everybody began to cheer loudly for them.

"State champs! State champs! State champs!" The students and staff were fired up.

After the cheering noise settled down, Principal Jumper presented another very tall basketball trophy and a state trophy as well. "We will display these trophies in our glass showcase," Principal Jumper stated to the school. "I have personal trophies for each member on our basketball team and Coach Wilson as well. One more thing. These four young men—Ice Cream, Fats, Range, and Deep—made a big impact on this team. Now I will turn it over to Coach Wilson. Thank you."

"Listen up. I've never coached a great basketball team like this one," Coach Wilson stated. "In my life, I've never seen four guys like Ice Cream, Fats, Range, and Deep make so many free throws. These four young men will be professional free throw shooters one day in the future. They are good now, shooting at 97 percent from the free throw line."

After the coach's speech, everybody began to cheer loudly.

"Anything you guys have to say?" Coach Wilson asked them.

"Sure, Coach," Ice Cream voiced out. He spoke clearly to the school. "We as a team thank you fans for your support for the whole year. Hopefully, for the next three years, we can win the state title three more times."

After the presentation and speeches were done, everyone was getting autographs and signatures from the dream boys. Then they all exited the gym and went back to class. The rest of the school day went very well for the dream boys and the girls as well. All the students and staff members could not wait until the next season.

Going into the dream boys' and girls' sophomore year, basketball season had come around again. All the students had made signs for the games to support their team. The dream boys were ready for the new season and trying to win another state title. When the season started, Coach Wilson's team had another undefeated season for the second year in a row. The dream boys had made winning free throws to advance to the state championship again. Coach Wilson's team had won the state title again for the second year in a row. Fats made the winning free throw shot to win the state title this year. Everybody rushed to the court to celebrate like last year's state title.

"We are number one! We are number one! We are number one!" The Swish High School students were fired up all over the court.

The news was all over the state saying that Coach Wilson's team had won two state titles. After the school year was over, during the summer months, some of the students made arrangements to see the dream boys work out at the gym. When their junior year began, the students began to cheer and make loud noises before the season started. The dream boys' goal in high school was to win four state titles in a row. So far, they had done it for two years, and it was getting better and better for them every year.

In the month of October, before the November season, Coach Blue and his wife plus the LA sports reporters arrived back to see the dream boys again. The LA reporters and the local sports reporters interviewed Coach Wilson and Coach Blue at the same time. All the other high schools could not get over how Ice Cream, Fats, Range, and Deep made their free throws under pressure like that. They did not know the dream boys had been shooting free throws like that since the first grade. Good Pass, Block, Dunk, and Set Shot were the most popular girls in Swish High School because of the dream boys' free throw skills and also how the boys carried themselves in school and out of school. Basketball season had arrived.

"Hey, Coach Wilson, we want to win the state again this year." The dream boys were steamed up in their minds.

"Sounds great, boys. Let's do it!" Coach Wilson responded.

Throughout the whole season, Coach Wilson's team won every game during regular season. The fantastic four made many free throw shots for their team.

"Okay, guys, listen up. Our first round state game is this Friday night," he declared. "Let's have a good practice these first four days."

"Yes, sir, Coach!" the whole team answered.

Monday through Thursday practice went great for Coach Wilson's team. Friday night arrived for the first round state game.

"Okay, guys, let's go out there and win this first round game," Coach Wilson voiced out to his team in the huddle.

The game was very close against this great high school team from out of the city. They were going into the last quarter with thirty-five seconds left with a tied score, sixty-eight to sixty-eight. Fats had the ball driving to the basket and was fouled.

"Okay, Fats, let's hit these free throws!" Block blurted out from the crowd.

"Yeah, Fats, knock it in!" Deep shouted.

Swish! Swish! Fats pounded his two free throws like butter.

"Yes, Fats!" Coach Wilson shouted out.

The other team rushed down the court with twenty-one seconds left and scored two points. Now the game was a tie again, seventy to seventy. Coach Wilson's team was coming up the court with twelve seconds left.

"Time out! Time out!" Coach Wilson shouted out to the official.

Both teams were in their huddles.

Coach Wilson planned a play for his team. "Hey, guys, let's set a high pick for Range. You get the ball from Deep, and you sprint to the basket on Ice Cream's side and go for the shot."

"Yes, sir, Coach!" Range responded.

The game horn sounded off for both teams to get back on the court.

"Okay, Range, go!" Coach Wilson shouted out to him. "Okay, Range! Good drive to the basket!"

Range was fouled to shoot two free throws.

"Yeah, Range, make these," Ice Cream voiced out softly, standing on one side around the free throw lane.

Swish! Swish! Range nailed both free throws. The score was seventy-two to seventy; Coach Wilson's team was winning with ten seconds left. The other team rushed back down the other end of the court to shoot and miss. Ice Cream grabbed the rebound; by that time, the game was over. Coach Wilson's team advanced to the second round, and Deep made the winning free throw for the game to advance to the final state game. Fats and Deep hit the clutch with free throws to win both rounds. All the sports reporters interviewed both Coach Wilson and Coach Blue. Coach Wilson's team won the state title again for the third year. Ice Cream was hitting the two winning free throws for that state title in the final championship game.

After the school year ended, the dream boys were ready for their last year, going into their senior year along with the girls. During the summer, going into their senior year, the dream boys practiced all summer long.

"Hey, man, these last three years have been great," Ice Cream voiced out to his free throw buddies.

"I know, man. This has been wonderful, man," Fats stated.

"Man, I am almost crying. Our dream goal is coming true to be free throw pros," Range affirmed.

The dream boys were resting on the court at their local gym.

"Hey, man. Coach Blue talked to my parents, man," Ice Cream divulged.

"What Coach Blue say?" Fats was fired up.

"Man, he wants us to play for his college team," Ice Cream declared.

"Oh, wow! Yes, sir, I am ready! Super news, man! I am ready!" Fats, Range, and Deep were steamed up with smiley faces.

"Guess what, man," Ice Cream voiced out.

"What? What?" Deep blurted out.

"If we go to the state finals and win again, Coach Blue will get a basketball company to sponsor us and the girls."

"Oh, nice, man! Yes, sir!" Fats, Range, and Deep were juiced up with joy in their hearts.

"Hey, man, let's practice some more free throws," Deep declared.

"Yes, sir," Ice Cream answered.

The boys rose up quickly to work on some more free throws to get better and better. The dream boys continued working on their free throws. They were shooting so great because of the opportunity Coach Blue had promised them about the basketball sponsorship.

"Ice Cream, man, I am so ready to win this state title four times, man," Deep voiced out to him.

"I know, man. Plus, we will be wearing company basketball gear after we finish high school," Ice Cream declared.

The dream boys practiced four days a week for four hours and taking water breaks. They worked out great until the last week before their last year in school. School time had come around, and the dream boys and the girls were very excited to finish plus try to win their fourth state title in a row. That first Monday morning at school, all the students made signs saying "Four State Titles in a Row." The dream boys were working out every day after school along with their teammates.

"Looking good, guys," Coach Wilson voiced out at practice.

When the season began, Coach Blue's team won all of their regular season games mostly from the free throw line. The dream boys made all of their free throws for Coach Wilson. Coach Wilson's team again advanced to the state championship game for the fourth time in a row, just like the dream boys had mentioned during their first year. Ice Cream hit the wining free throw shot by one point higher to win the state championship game, closing out their last season at Swiss High School.

"I can't believe it, man!" Range voiced out to his boys.

"Yes, sir, man! We did it!" Ice Cream blurted out loudly.

Fats and Deep were crying from their hearts along with the girls and parents. All the celebration continued at Swiss High School. The local and LA sports reporters were staying around, interviewing Coach Wilson and Coach Blue.

"Coach Wilson, how does it feel to have four state championship titles in a row?" the sports reporters asked.

"I feel like a new man who's made history for life," He answered. "I've never experience such great players since I began teaching basketball. Also, I've never seen four boys who can shoot free throws at 97 percent that young in life."

"It's amazing to see these four boys shoot free throws like that," the sports reporters responded. "Thank you, Coach Wilson." The sports reporters approached Coach Blue. "Hey, Coach, this has been a great four years for Coach Wilson's team, winning four state titles. Give me your input about this team."

"Well, first of all, this team has done great all four years. Also, those four boys I've known for a while are great free throw shooters. Ice Cream, Fats, Range, and Deep—I met them at the ice cream store back in their community when they were small teenagers. These guys can shoot free throws like butter. I am a witness to that. One day these four young men will be professional free throw shooters in life. I just have that feeling about that," Coach Blue affirmed.

"Who taught these boys how to shoot free throws like that?" the sports reporters asked.

"Well, the boys told me they have been shooting free throws since the first grade by starting out with paper balls into the trash can."

"Wow! That's amazing, Coach!" The sports reporters' faces were elated. "Thank you, Coach Blue." The reporters departed.

Coach Wilson's Swiss High School basketball team made history, winning four state championships in a row. Every city in the state and every high school was amazed that Coach Wilson's basketball team won four state titles in a row. All the residents in every city talked about were Ice Cream, Fats, Range, and Deep making their free throws with the game on the line under pressure. There were a lot of write-ups in the newspaper about Coach Wilson's four state championships. He was voted the best high school coach in the state. Many universities wanted Coach Wilson to coach their basketball teams. Swiss High School made a lot of money by winning games in the last four years. The school purchased many new things for the students and repaired some things at the school for the future.

The rest of the school year went great for the dream boys and the girls. When the month of June came around, it was time for graduation. The dream boys and the girls began to get their things together for next year of college at USC. The students and coaches as well as staff members went up to the dream boys to thank them for four years of winning the state title. The day before graduation, the principal released all the seniors early, around 11:00 a.m., to go home and prepare themselves for graduation day. The dream boys and the girls stopped by the ice cream store on their way home.

"Hey, ladies and champs, come on in. My treat to you all—a cone of ice cream!" the store manager stated to the dream boys and their girlfriends.

They were sitting at their same tables, talking about old times, how they were shooting paper balls and met Coach Blue and his wife. The customers were taking pictures of the dream boys because of them winning the state titles.

"Hey, guys, I am tired," Good Pass voiced out to the crew.

"Me too." They all agreed.

They all exited the ice cream store to go home for graduation day tomorrow. Early the next morning, the dream boys and the girls got out of their beds with smiles on their faces.

"Hey, Mom, me and the guys will practice some free throws at the court," Ice Cream voiced out.

"Okay, son. Do not stay too long. You have to get ready for graduation," his mother stated.

"The girls might go with us too," Ice Cream voiced out again to his mother.

"Okay, boy. Those girls love to hang with you guys all the time, I see," she responded.

"Yes, Mother. They love it just like we do," Ice Cream declared.

After Ice Cream ate his breakfast, he called Fats, Range, and Deep.

"Hey, Fats, you ate breakfast?" Ice Cream asked.

"Yeah, man," Fats answered.

"Great! Let's go to the court around 12:30 p.m. and practice some free throws," Ice Cream stated.

"Yes, sir, Cream! I am ready, man," Fats responded.

"Okay, sounds good," Ice Cream responded. "I will call Range and Deep too."

"Okay, Cream. I'll see you out there," Fats responded.

"Hey, Range."

"Hey, Cream," Range answered.

"Look, man, I talked to Fats. We want to practice shooting free throws at the court around 12:30 p.m.," Ice Cream voiced out to him on the phone.

"Yes, sir, Cream! I am ready to go," Range answered.

"Okay, great. I'll see you out there," Ice Cream responded. Ice Cream connected with Deep. "Hey, Deep, how are you doing, brother?"

"I am doing good, man," Deep answered.

"Hey, look, Deep, I talked to Fats and Range. We are going to practice some free throws at the court at around 12:30 p.m.," Ice Cream announced to him on the phone.

"Sounds like a great plan. I am ready, man!" Deep shouted out.

"Okay, I'll see you out there," Ice Cream voiced out to him.

"Sure, Cream," Deep answered.

At 12:30 p.m., the boys met at the court to practice their free throw shots for two hours. Around 3:00 p.m., the fantastic four went back home to prepare for high school graduation. The girls had called the boys, thinking they were home at around 11:45 a.m. The parents told the girls that those boys had eaten fast and rushed out to the court to shoot free throws. The girls had an idea that they would do that. The dream boys made sure they got some practice in that day to be more ready for college basketball.

Later on, they all met at the high school at 6:00 p.m. for graduation. The graduation went very well; the school was packed all the way from top to bottom. When the senior class began to walk in, the people began the cheer very loudly. They began to cheer out, saying "Four state titles!" multiple times for thirty seconds. After the cheers settled down, the principal opened up his speech, welcoming everybody, and then right away, he was talking about those dream boys. He talked about how they had made those pressure clutch winning free throws at the end of the ball games to bring them four state titles. Coach Wilson, in his speech, was saying to all the people that he had never seen four boys who were 97 percent from the line at a young age and could make so many in a row. People were taking pictures of the senior class but of the dream boys mostly. After graduation was over, the dream boys and the girls and their parents went back home to finish the celebration.

"Listen up, guys and girls. Congratulations on receiving your high school diplomas today," the parents stated.

"Thank you very much," the dream boys and the girls responded.

"Also, Coach Blue will call you guys to prepare you all for college at USC in LA," the parents also stated.

After the graduation day party had come to an end, starting the next day, the dream boys worked on their free throws very hard for the whole summer months.

Chapter 12

ATTEND COLLEGE

Around the first week of August, Coach Blue called each parent to make arrangements to fly the dream boys and the girls off to USC by that Friday. Early that week, the dream boys and the girls packed their things for college. Everybody met at Ice Cream's house on Friday morning at seven o'clock to prepare to leave at 8:00 a.m. for their local airport. The dream boys and girls' flight was scheduled to leave at 10:00 a.m. for LA.

"Okay, everyone, let's load up to go. We can't be late," Deep's parents voiced out at Ice Cream's house.

They all left and arrived at the airport's gate area. When 9:30 a.m. came around, the parents hugged their children and said their goodbyes. After the hugs and cries, the dream boys and the girls exited for the plane to their assigned seats. While the fantastic four and the girls were flying to Southern California, Coach Blue and his wife were getting prepared to meet them at the LA airport. It was 1:00 p.m., West Coast time, when the crew landed in LA but 5:00 p.m., Eastern Time, back home. At the arrival gate, Coach Blue and his wife met the crew, who were walking inside the LA airport.

"Hey, Coach! Mrs. Blue!" Ice Cream, Fats, Range, and Deep shouted.

"Hey, Coach! Mrs. Blue!" the girls shouted out as well.

"Hey, guys!" Coach Blue and his wife answered.

After all the hugs were finished, they exited to the baggage claim area.

"Hey, Coach, we are ready to play for USC," Deep blurted out.

"Yeah, Coach!" Ice Cream, Fats, and Range voiced out too.

"I know, guys. I can't wait myself," Coach Blue responded. "Hey, guys, call your parents to let them know you all made it here safely. The phones are over there."

"Okay, Coach. Will do." The crew walked over to the phones to call.

After the dream boys and the girls called home, they all exited to Coach Blue's van, going to the college campus.

"Hey, Ice Cream, Fats, Range, and Deep, we have great players on our team."

"Okay, Coach. Great!" the boys responded.

"Listen up. There is one thing to improve on, guys."

"What's that, Coach?" the boys voiced out.

"Our team free throw percentage is not good," Coach Blue stated.

"Wow, Coach!" the dream boys blurted out loud.

"I am glad you guys are here to help our team free throw percentage," Coach Blue elated.

"We will do our best," Deep responded.

"Yes, sir, Deep!" Ice Cream declared.

After Coach Blue talked to the fantastic four about the team free throw percentage, they arrived at the USC campus.

"Hey, guys, I will take you to your dorm rooms."

"Okay, Coach Blue," the dream boys replied.

"My wife will take the girls to their dorm rooms," he declared.

"Okay, ladies, follow me." Mrs. Blue directed the girls.

"Okay, Mrs. Blue," the girls answered.

After they all checked out both the men's and women's dorms, they exited to the van, going to the arena. When they all arrived there and approached the court, the rest of the team were waiting there with the assistant coaches.

"Hey, everyone, these four young men are your new teammates." Coach Blue introduced the dream boys. "These four young men can shoot free throws very well."

"Okay, Coach Blue," they answered.

"Listen up, fellows. My wife and I are going to show them around the college and where their classes will be," Coach Blue verbalized to his team and coaches.

"Okay, Coach," they answered.

While Coach Blue and his wife were making rounds with the young crew, Coach Blue was instructing the fantastic four about practice on Monday after class. It was getting late on that Friday evening at the arena. Coach Blue sped up their routes, and it was time for them to head back to the dorm to unpack their things. The other teammates as well as the assistant coaches realized the fantastic four would help them win games by making free throws. They began talking about how the dream boys could also help them have a chance for the final four and win the championship. The dream boys and the girls began to unpack their things in their rooms.

"Hey, listen up, ladies and gentlemen!" Coach Blue was fired up with his new players. "My wife and I want to thank you all again for selecting USC."

"No problem, Coach!" The dream boys and the girls were thrilled.

Coach Blue voiced out his closing remarks. "Okay, you all, it is 9:00 p.m. My wife and I have to leave and get some rest."

"Okay, Coach Blue," the crew responded.

"Call your parents and let them know everything is in order," Coach Blue vocalized.

"Okay, Coach Blue," the crew answered.

"Good night, guys," Coach Blue and his wife voiced out, and they left the campus.

"Good night, Coach Blue and Mrs. Blue," the crew answered back.

The fantastic four and their girlfriends called their parents to let them know everything was good. Early Saturday morning, the dream boys and the girls made a lot of friends on campus all day and night. Most of the students had heard about them and seen on LA sports news the fantastic four shoot free throws at 97 percent. The crew had been busy talking to students outside on campus about the upcoming basketball season.

"Hey, guys, let's take a break under this tree," Range and Deep voiced out.

"Yes, that sound goods," Block and Dunk responded.

They all rested for a while under the big tree.

A large crowd of students spoke to the crew. "Hey, guys, how are you all doing?"

"We are good, just resting for a while," Set Shot voiced out.

"Cool," the students answered. "We have seen you four guys shoot free throws on television. Thank for playing basketball here at USC. You guys are awesome at the free throw line." The students were steamed up about the upcoming season.

"Thank you all," the fantastic four responded.

"We lost a lot of games at the free throw line last year," one student voiced out.

"Yes, I heard that from our coach," Ice Cream stated.

"Yes, we can't wait to see you guys shoot free throws in the game next season!" Another student was juiced up with joy.

"Thank you. We will do our best," Deep responded.

"Okay. Have a great day!" The students departed from the young crew.

"Man, these students love us already," Fats stated.

"Yeah, man. We have to bring our free throw game to help win games and the final four championship," Ice Cream declared.

"Yes, you boys do," Good Pass retorted.

"Hey, everybody, let's call it a day," Range vocalized to the crew.

"Yes, Range, I agree," Block stated.

They all walked back to their dorm rooms to say good night. Early Sunday morning, around ten o'clock, the dream boys ate breakfast.

"Hey, man, I will call Coach Blue to ask him if we can practice at the arena's practice gym," Ice Cream announced to his teammates.

"Yeah, Cream. Sounds like a great idea," Deep responded.

The dream boys walked over to the pay phone.

"Good morning, Coach," Ice Cream voiced out on the phone. "Can we practice our free throws today?"

"Sure, son. I will let the rest of the team know as well," Coach Blue answered. "I will meet everybody at the same spot with the game bus on campus at around 3:00 p.m."

"Okay, Coach. I will let the rest of the boys know, and our girlfriends want to come and watch us practice," Ice Cream mentioned.

"Sure, Cream. The rest of the team will bring their lady friends too. That's fine," Coach responded.

"Thank you, Coach," Ice Cream answered.

"Okay, Cream. See you all there." Coach Blue finished his end of the conversation.

"Okay, Coach. Thank you very much. See you soon." Ice Cream hung up the phone.

When 2:55 p.m. came around, all the team players and their girlfriends met at the spot on campus, waiting on Coach Blue. Coach Blue and his wife arrived at the spot right at 3:00 p.m. with the game bus.

"Hey, everybody. You all ready for practice?" Coach Blue voiced out to his team players.

"Yes, Coach Blue. We are ready," they responded.

At 3:45 p.m., they all arrived at the arena for a two-hour shoot-around practice. The team players walked inside the arena to the locker room to change into their practice gear.

"Ten minutes, guys. Meet me on the court," Coach Blue stated.

The girlfriends and Coach Blue's wife went straight to the court to have their seats. Ten minutes later, the team arrived on the court, and the girlfriends and Coach Blue's wife began to cheer for them.

"Hey, guys, huddle up in the center circle of the court," Coach Blue directed. "Listen up. Let's welcome our new four team members—Ice Cream, Fats, Range, and Deep. The first thing we will do is warm up with some running drills."

The dream boys were in great shape while running those drills. Actually, the fantastic four wanted to get at the free throw line to shoot. When shoot-around time arrived, the team split into groups of four players to a basket to shoot free throws. Certainly, the dream boys went to one basket to start shooting their free throws.

"Okay, guys, listen up. We have to do better next season at the free throw line," Coach Blue deliberated to his team. "Our team percentage was not that good last year at 68 percent, but we want to get better this year on out. We have one hour of practice left. Let's shoot fifty free throws, and give me your count."

Ice Cream began to shoot his fifty free throws first in his group.

"Wow, man, look at Cream shoot!" His teammate from the other group of players at their basket noticed.

"I see, man. He can shoot free throws great," his group teammate responded.

All of a sudden, the entire group at each basket began to stare at the dream boys shooting their free throws.

"Hey! Hey! The rest of you guys focus on your free throws at your own basket!" Coach Blue indicated.

"Sorry, Coach," they answered.

"Man, they will absolutely help us win some games and have a chance for the final four tournament." A nearby teammate was fired up, whispering to another with joy.

"Yes, sir, for sure," his shooting partner responded.

After shoot-around time was over, that same group of teammates approached Ice Cream, Fats, Range, and Deep while walking back to the locker room.

"Hey, Cream, how long you guys been shooting free throws like that?" they asked.

"Since the first grade," Fats answered.

"Wow, that's amazing, guys!" They were overjoyed.

"You guys will help us for sure next season," one teammate declared.

"We will do our best to help our team," Deep voiced out.

"Thank you, guys, for your support," Range stated.

They all finished changing back to their regular clothes and exited the locker room to head to Coach Blue.

"Hey, everybody, give me your free throw count," Coach Blue voiced out to his players.

The other teammates' percentages were at 78 percent to 85 percent, and the dream boys' percentages were at 99%.

"I am impressed, fellows. Your free throws are improving. Great job, guys!" Coach Blue was fired up with joy. "Listen up, fellows. If we keep these percentages up, we can have a chance at the final four tournament." Coach Blue was juiced up with a smiley face.

"Yes, sir, Coach!" All the players were steamed up and ready.

"Okay, guys, let's head back to campus," he stated.

They were all back on the bus, riding home.

"Okay, guys, we are here. Great practice, fellows. Also, get ready for class on Monday," Coach Blue declared.

"Okay, Coach," they all responded.

Coach Blue and his wife left with the bus, heading home. The team players and their girlfriends except the dream boys and their girlfriends hung around the campus lobby.

"Okay, guys, we will see you all in class on Monday," the other players voiced out to the dream boys.

"Okay, fellows," the dream boys responded.

The dream boys and the girls rested in the campus lobby for a few minutes.

"Hey, there is a McDonald's across the highway. Let's go eat there," Ice Cream vocalized.

"Sounds great," Block responded.

They all arrived at the McDonald's and purchased their dinner meals to eat there.

Some college students approached the dream boys and the girls at their table. "Hi, guys. How are you all doing?"

"Hello," the crew answered.

"We saw you four guys with your basketballs," the students mentioned.

"Yes, we love to shoot free throws," Fats voiced out.

"Okay. You all must be the four players everyone on campus is talking about," one student affirmed.

"I guess you can say that we're just shooters," Range responded.

"How long you guys been shooting free throws?" another student asked.

"They have been shooting since the first grade," Good Pass declared.

"Oh, wow! That's great. You guys will help us win a lot of games next season for sure," the students responded.

"Hope so," Range voiced out.

"What are you all guys' names?" one student asked.

"My name is Ice Cream. This is my girlfriend, Good Pass," Ice Cream introduced.

"My name is Fats. This is my girlfriend, Block," Fats introduced.

"My name is Range. This is my girlfriend, Dunk," Range introduced.

"My name is Deep. This is my girlfriend, Set Shot," Deep introduced.

"Nice, guys!" the students responded. "Okay. See you all at school and at the games." The students departed.

"Okay. Nice meeting you all," the dream boys and girls replied.

"Man, I am tired from practice today. Let's call it a night!" Deep voiced out.

"Yeah, guys. I am ready too," Dunk declared.

They all finished their meals and began walking back to campus. The time was getting late, so they said good night to one another to be ready for class on Monday.

Chapter 13

FINAL FOUR CHAMPIONSHIPS

Early Monday morning, starting off their freshman year at USC, the crew arrived at their classes. Obviously, while changing classes, they met up at the same class. Three months passed by. The time had come around for basketball season, with the boys going into the first day of basketball practice. A few USC students hung around after class to watch the basketball team practice for a few minutes.

"Hey, guys, let's have a free throw practice for the rest of the week," Coach Blue advised his team. "Let's break off into fours at each basket to shoot ten free throws each."

As Coach Blue walked to each basket, looking at his shooters, he was very cheerful. Deep began his shooting practice.

"Good free throw shooting, Range!" Coach was fired up. "Yes, sir, Deep!" Coach was pleased. "You next, Fats," Coach blurted out while Deep finished up his last shot.

Fats approached the free throw line to start.

"Okay, Fats! That's what I am talking about, man!" Coach shouted.

Fats finished up his ten free throws, followed by Ice Cream.

"Nice, Ice Cream!" Coach was overjoyed. "Nice, fellows! Keep it up!" Coach Blue was walking away, leaving their baskets. "Hey, guys, looking good down there!"

Coach Blue had his eyes down the court and noticed his other players shooting. Coach Blue's free throw practice went very well all week, along with his regular practices. During the month of November, the first game was getting close. The sports news reporters and other local media arrived at USC to interview Coach Blue about last year's season and this new season.

"Coach, tell us the reason your team lost so many games last year to get knocked out the NCAA tournament," the sports reporters asked.

"Our free throw percentage last year was not that good at 58 percent," Coach Blue answered. "This year, I have four new players on my team. They are great free throw shooters. I can't wait until the next opening game against UCLA."

"Okay, Coach. That's awesome! Wish you well," the sports reporters responded.

"Thank you, sir," Coach Blue replied.

When that Friday of the interview week came around, Coach Blue's team had just had a shoot-around practice for their first home game on Saturday evening.

"Okay, fellows, huddle up," Coach Blue voiced out to his team. "Our game is at 3:00 p.m. tomorrow. I will be at the campus to pick you all up at 1:00 p.m. Get dressed and load up on the game bus to head back to campus," Coach Blue directed.

"Yes, sir, Coach!" the team answered.

While they were all riding back to campus, Coach Blue was explaining his game plan. "Okay, guys. We are here. Make sure you all get a good night's rest tonight," Coach Blue declared. "I'll see you all here and your girlfriends at the spot tomorrow."

"Okay, Coach," they all responded.

Early Saturday morning, around eight o'clock, the crew walked to the McDonald's across the highway for breakfast.

"This food is good," Fats voiced out.

"Yeah, man, it is," Deep responded.

"Man, this is our first college game," Ice Cream expressed.

"Yes, fellows. Be ready to shoot your free throws at pressure points," Block mentioned.

"You are so right, Block," Set Shot responded.

"Yes, fellows. Your free throw games have to be on fire," Good Pass stated.

"Yes, Good Pass. I agree," Dunk declared.

"Hey, everybody, let's finish this breakfast and be back at our rooms by 10:00 a.m.," Range affirmed.

The ten o'clock hour had arrived, and the crew arrived at their rooms, preparing for the first game. The dream boys were just relaxing, lying across their beds, face up with their basketballs, twirling them in the air, working on their shooting forms.

"Hey, guys, I think I will take a short nap," Fats voiced out.

"That sounds good, Fats," Ice Cream responded.

Range and Deep reacted. "Yeah, that sounds good, Ice Cream and Fats."

After one hour passed by, Ice Cream slowly cracked his eyes open; the fantastic four slept until almost noon.

"Hey, wake up, guys! It is twelve in the afternoon. Man, Coach Blue will be here at 1:00 p.m.!" Ice Cream blurted out loud.

"Oh man, I was sleeping good, man," Deep retorted.

Fats woke up from his nap. "Man, my body is stiff right now."

"Hey, stiff Fats, my brother, it is almost game time. Get ready to shoot free throws," Ice Cream stated.

The dream boys began to get dressed along with their teammates plus all their girlfriends. They all met Coach Blue and his wife at the meeting spot at exactly 1:00 p.m.

"Good afternoon, everyone," Coach Blue and his wife vocalized to everybody.

"Good afternoon, Coach Blue and Mrs. Blue," they all responded.

"You guys ready to play?" Coach Blue voiced out to his players.

"Yes, sir, Coach!" the team responded.

"Okay, let's load up on the game bus and head to the basketball arena," Coach Blue declared.

Fifteen minutes later, they arrived at the USC basketball arena.

"Wow, man, there's a lot of cars out here." Range was stunned.

"Yeah, Range, for sure. There's a lot people here," Set Shot blurted out.

"Look at the long lines at the main entrance doors," Block voiced out.

"Okay, guys, let's head to the locker room, and my wife will lead the ladies to the arena to take their seats," Coach Blue directed.

All the family members plus the dream boys' and their girlfriends' first-grade teacher, Mrs. Hoops, tuned into the game back in Virginia.

"Okay, guys, let's go out here and win this game against UCLA!" Coach Blue was steamed up.

"Yes, sir, Coach!" the team responded.

At 2:30 p.m., both teams exited their locker rooms, arriving at the court to warm up. When Coach Blue's USC team arrived on the court, the fans began to cheer very loudly. After the warmup period ended, the game was ready to start. Both teams rushed back to their benches into their team huddles.

"Okay, guys, this is it. Let's win this game!" Coach Blue was fired up. "Okay, here are my starters—Ice Cream, Fats, Range, Deep, and Dion," Coach Blue directed.

As the game began, UCLA was leading almost the whole game until the last five minutes. The score was sixty-seven to fifty-seven, with UCLA winning so far.

"Time out! Time out!" Coach Blue shouted. "Hey, fellows, our outside shots are not going in. Let's continue to run our offense and draw some fouls. We have five minutes to come back and win this game at the free throw line. Let's give the ball to Fats first. He will drive to the basket and draw a foul first," Coach Blue voiced out in the huddle.

"Okay, Coach," Fats responded.

"The next time down, Range will do the same," he continued.

"Okay, Coach," Range responded.

"Then after that, the next time down, Ice Cream will do the same thing," he also indicated.

"Okay, Coach!" Ice Cream responded.

The game horn sounded off to continue the last five minutes to play. The USC team had the ball, and Ice Cream passed it to Fats.

"Drive, Fats! Drive to the basket!" Deep shouted.

Fats was quickly driving to the basket, and he got a foul. Fats had two free throws to shoot. *Swish! Swish!* He made them both.

"Yes, Fats, yes!" Coach Blue was juiced up with joy along with their teammates.

USC was coming back, sixty-seven to fifty-nine, with four minutes and ten seconds left to play. USC was playing good defense to stop UCLA from scoring. Block was looking very happy about her man Fats making those two free throws. The USC team had the basketball again. Deep received the pass from Fats, and he chest-passed it to Dion. Range came off the low screen from Ice Cream, and Dion passed the ball to Range in the left corner. Range noticed an open-lane drive to the basket. He took off hard, driving toward the basket, and was fouled by a UCLA player.

"Yes, Range, yes!" Dunk, overjoyed, stood from her seat. "Range has to make these two free throws," Dunk voiced out to the girls.

Range approached the free throw line and made both free throws with no problem.

"Yes, Range, yes!" Dunk shouted again.

"Yes, Range! Great free throw shots!" Coach Blue and the teammates shouted from the bench.

The USC fans had been cheering very loudly for the last five minutes. Coach Blue's USC team was coming back closer, sixty-seven to sixty-one. USC really shut down UCLA's offense, with no shots made in the last five minutes. With under three minutes to play, USC had the basketball. Deep received a cross-court pass from Fats, and he split the double team from two UCLA players, driving to the basket, and was fouled.

"That's what I am talking about, honey! Draw that foul!" Set Shot blurted out.

Deep had two free throw shots to help bring his team score closer. Deep approached the free throw line with two minutes and forty-five seconds left to play. Set Shot was standing up, watching his free throw dynamics. Deep tossed his first free throw shot up and swished it through the net. His second free throw swished through the net again. Set Shot jumped for joy after both free throws. USC was coming back closer, with the score being sixty-seven to sixty-three. UCLA had not yet scored these last two minutes because of the amazing defense of Coach Blue's USC team. The UCLA coach called a timeout to figure out what was wrong with his guys. Both teams rushed off the court to their benches.

"Hey, guys, you all looking good out there." Coach Blue was pleased with his team. "We have two minutes and twenty seconds left, and we are just down four points to tie this game. Listen up, guys. Run your regular offense to set up a play for Dion to shoot a bank shot off the glass."

The game horn sounded off for both teams to get back on the court to play. UCLA had the basketball, working on getting a shot made for the last two minutes. The USC team was doing it again, stopping UCLA from scoring. Coach Blue's USC team had received the ball back down their end, and Dion made the bank shot off the glass. The score was now sixty-seven to sixty-five, with one minute and fifty-seven seconds left to play. Coach Blue's team was pressing full court and had stolen the basketball back. Ice Cream had the ball, driving hard to the basket, and was fouled by a UCLA player. Ice Cream had two free throws with one minute and thirty-five seconds left. He made both free throws with no problem.

"Yes, Ice Cream!" Good Pass shouted out.

"Yes, sir, Cream!" Coach Blue was steamed up along with the teammates.

The score was a tie with one minute and nineteen seconds left. UCLA had the basketball, still trying to score; also, their coach was very upset with his team's performance. There was no score again by UCLA with forty-five seconds left. USC had the basketball, with Range bringing it down across the half-court line.

"Time out!" Coach Blue blurted out to the official.

Both teams rushed to their benches.

"Okay, guys, great job coming back to tie this game." Coach Blue was overjoyed with his team. "Listen up, guys. Fats will drive to the basket to draw a foul and shoot two free throws. Fats, make these two free throws and bring us home with a win."

"Yes, sir, Coach!" Fats responded.

The game horn sounded off, and both teams were back on the court. Ice Cream had the basketball, approaching the left side, where Fats was. Fats broke open and received the pass from Ice Cream. Fats began to drive to the basket and was fouled by another UCLA player with five seconds left on the game clock. He had two free throws to shoot.

"Okay, Fats, baby—let's get it, man!" Block shouted out.

Fats approached the free throw line and made both shots with a swish.

"Yeah, Fats! That's what I am talking about!" Block was overjoyed.

"Yes, sir, Fats! Good free throws!" Coach Blue and his bench players shouted out.

The score was now sixty-seven to sixty-nine; Coach Blue's team had advanced the lead. The UCLA team rushed down the court to score, but time had run out. The game horn sounded off, and the game was over. Coach Blue's team came back to win their first game of the season. USC fans rushed to the court to help celebrate the victory over UCLA. After the celebrating, Coach Blue's team began approaching their locker room.

"Hey, guys, great job coming back plus great defense to win this game!" Coach Blue voiced out to his team. "Great free throw shooting also, guys. Let's keep this pace up, fellows. We can make it to the final four this year!"

"Okay, Coach. Let's do it!" the whole team responded.

The rest of the season went great for Coach Blue's USC team. They advanced to the final four championship game against North Carolina.

"Okay, guys, great season. We have made it here tonight to win this national title against a great shooting North Carolina team," Coach Blue verbalized.

While both teams were warming up for the game to start, the girls were very nervous about the North Carolina team winning tonight. The game horn sounded off, and both teams rushed to their benches.

"Okay, guys, this is it. We have all been waiting for this moment to win our first championship title," Coach Blue indicated to his team.

The game horn sounded off again, and the five starting players for both teams arrived at the jump circle at center court. North Carolina won the toss, approaching their basket, and scored two points. Coach Blue's team received the ball; teammate Dion scored two points for USC. The game was close all the way up to one minute left before halftime. The score was a tie at the half. Both teams rushed to their locker rooms.

"Okay, guys, we are hanging on to this game. Keep up the defense—and great free throws!" Coach Blue was pleased with his team's performance.

"Hey, everybody—let's win this championship title, man!" Deep stated to his teammates in the locker room.

"Listen up, guys. Huddle up," Coach Blue directed. "In this third quarter, let's keep these free throws going in the basket, fellows."

The third quarter began, and both teams were still battling to win. The dream boys were still making their free throws like butter. The third quarter came to a close with the score fifty-eight to fifty-four, USC up by four points. Both teams were at their benches for instructions from their coaches to start the fourth and last quarter.

"Okay, guys, let's continue to the lead all the way out the fourth quarter and win this title." Coach Blue was steamed up.

"Yes, sir, Coach!" The team was fired up with good spirit.

The game horn sounded off; both teams approached the court to start the last quarter. USC had the basketball on their end. Ice Cream was at the top of the key with the ball, looking for Range to cut off from the stream play. Ice Cream passed the ball to Range, and he was fouled by a Carolina player.

"Okay, Range, you know what to do!" Dunk shouted out from her seat.

Range made both free throws, all swish shots. The score was now sixty to fifty-four with six minutes and forty-five seconds left to play. Coach Blue's team was pulling away, just like he had said at the end of the third quarter. North Carolina received the ball back on their end and made two points. They were pressing full court after every basket they made. Carolina came up with a steal off the press and made two points. Before the press from Carolina, the score was sixty to fifty-six; now it had changed to sixty to fifty-eight after Carolina's steal.

"Time out!" Coach Blue shouted out to the official near him. "Hey, guys, what happened out there? Stay focused. We had a six-point lead at the six-minute mark. Let's get this lead back!"

The game horn sounded off; both teams were back on the court. The girls and parents were looking a little sad. They were getting chills and thinking about who would win this title with three minutes and thirty seconds left. USC had the ball, Fats controlling the offense. Deep set a pick for Ice Cream; he received the ball and then made a hard drive on the left side toward the basket. He under-passed the ball to Range, and he was fouled.

"Nice pass, Cream!" Coach Blue shouted out to him.

"Come on, Range! Hit these free throws, buddy!" Dunk blurted out.

Range made both free throws with no problem.

"Yes, sir, Range!" his teammates sitting on the bench shouted.

The score was sixty-two to fifty-eight, USC still holding on to the lead, with 1:75 seconds left to play in this final four championship game. North Carolina received the ball and made two points to cut USC's lead down to sixty-two to sixty with one minute and nineteen seconds left. North Carolina pressed full court and stole the ball from USC and made two points again. The score was now sixty-two to sixty-two with twenty-five seconds left.

"Time out! Time out!" Coach Blue shouted. "Okay, guys, listen up. We have twenty-five seconds left to play. Let's do this. Dion, you have the ball at the top of the key. Ice Cream, set a high screen at the free throw line right corner area for Deep. Deep, you come off that screen, cutting hard to the basket. Dion will pass you the ball while cutting off that screen and create a foul. Fats, you and Range take your man all the way weak side out of the play to give space for Deep."

"Okay, Coach," Range and Fats responded.

"Okay, one more thing—run your regular red offense until ten seconds and then start the play," Coach Blue instructed.

"Okay, Coach," his five starting guys responded.

The game horn sounded off. Both teams were back on the court; with twenty-five seconds remaining, USC had the basketball. USC was running their red offense, Ice Cream directing his teammates and watching the game clock.

"Okay, let's go, guys!" Coach Blue blurted out to his team with eleven seconds left.

Dion received the ball from Ice Cream at the top of the key. Ice Cream set the high screen for Deep, and he cut off and received the pass from Dion.

"Go, Deep, Go!" Coach Blue shouted out to Deep.

Deep was driving hard and fast to the basket and made the floater shot with the foul from a Carolina defender player at seven seconds left.

"Yes! Yes! Yes, Deep!" Set Shot shouted with joy from her seat.

The other girls and parents plus all the USC students were celebrating already.

"Yes, Deep! Great job!" Coach Blue was fired up.

The bench teammates were cheering and jumping up and down. Ice Cream, Fats, Dion, and Range were giving Deep high fives on the court. Deep approached the free throw line to shoot one free throw shot. The score was sixty-four to sixty-two with seven seconds left, USC still holding that lead. Coach Blue could taste a championship title for the first time during the dream boys' freshman year. Deep was at the free throw line with great confidence and made the free throw with a swish.

"Yes! Yes!" Coach Blue shouted.

Carolina rushed the ball down the court, trying to score with a foul like USC had done. No good chance for Carolina—time had run out, and the game was over. The final score was sixty-five to sixty-two; USC's basketball team were the final four champions. Everybody for USC rushed to the court to celebrate the victory. Coach Blue couldn't believe it; neither could all the students. The girls were hugging their dream boys, and their parents were crying their hearts out. USC's basketball team were cheering and jumping around, celebrating as well. Coach Blue made all his speeches during the ceremony. Deep was made MVP of that game.

After the season was over, the dream boys continued their free throw workout going into their sophomore year. The fantastic four's sophomore year had arrived, and they were ready for another final four title—hopefully. The season had begun, and USC's first game was against Texas Tech University.

"Hey, guys, welcome back to school. We had a great season last year, winning the title," Coach Blue stated. "Let's try and reach our goal to win four final four championships."

"Coach, that would be awesome," Ice Cream voiced out.

"Yeah, Cream. Man, that's history!" Deep shouted out.

"Listen up, fellows. Good practice today—and keep up our 96 percent free throw percentage," Coach Blue indicated.

"That is awesome, Coach!" Fats and Range voiced out.

"Okay, guys. Saturday, we have Texas Tech for our opening game here at home," he announced. "Also, guys, be here no later than 1:00 p.m. on Saturday."

"Yes, sir, Coach!" the whole team responded.

When Saturday arrived, Coach Blue's team was on time, right at 1:00 p.m. They all exited to their team locker room to get changed for the game. The arena was packed to the walls with people; plus, everybody wanted to see USC's team shoot those free throws again this season.

"Okay, guys, listen up. Texas Tech is a good free-throw-shooting and outside-shooting team," Coach Blue stated. "Let's focus on our shots and continue good free throw shooting."

Coach Blue's team arrived on the court with Texas Tech to warm up before the game started. The game horn sounded off, and both teams rushed to their benches for instructions from their coaches.

"Okay, guys, let's get out here and show Texas Tech we are the champs!" Coach Blue was steamed up.

"Yes, sir, Coach!" his starters responded.

Coach Blue had one starter, Dion, who had finished college. His new starter was Marvin, a six-foot-two point guard. The game horn sounded off; both teams arrived at the jump circle. USC won the toss and made two points from Ice Cream. Texas Tech rushed back down their end to set up a screen play and made two points as well. The game was running close all the way to the end of the first quarter—seventeen to twenty, Texas Tech leading. All of the first quarter, the dream boys were shooting free throws at a very high rate, 90 percent. Both teams were at their benches, getting ready for the second quarter to start.

"Okay, guys, let's stay focused on our defense and keep making our free throws and outside shots. One more thing—your outside shots need a little more arch," Coach Blue instructed.

"Okay, Coach," the starters responded.

The game horn sounded off to begin the second quarter. USC had the ball, passing it around to one another for an open shot.

"Good give-and-go, Ice Cream and Fats!" Coach Blue shouted out.

Fats was fouled on the give-and-go play. He had two free throws to shoot. Fats made both free throws to pull his team within one point.

"Yes, Fats, darling!" Block shouted out to her man.

The score was now nineteen to twenty, Texas Tech still up one point, with six minutes and forty-five seconds left before halftime. Texas Tech received the ball back, running their high offense play.

"Okay, fellows, keep passing the ball around fast!" the Texas Tech head coach blurted out from his bench. "Great shot, Jimmy!"

Coach Blue's USC team were coming down their end, pushing the basketball to Ice Cream.

"Set it up, guys!" Coach Blue supervised his team.

Ice Cream was looking to his right but passing the ball left to Deep. Deep received the pass and was driving hard to the basket to shoot and create a foul; plus, he made the shot.

"Good play, guys!" Coach Blue was elated at his bench.

Deep had two free throws to shoot and made both of them easily.

"Yes, Deep, yes!" Set Shot shouted from her seat.

"Yes, sir, brother! Good free throws!" Coach Blue was steamed up.

USC took the lead, twenty-three to twenty-two, with three minutes and fifteen seconds left before halftime. Both teams were really making baskets this whole first half, and the dream boys were making their free throws very well from the start of the game. With under one minute left before the half, Ice Cream was fouled, and he made his two free throws like they were nothing. In the last three minutes, the score had increased from twenty-three to twenty-two to thirty-eight to forty-two. The USC team was leading by four points now at the halftime period.

"Hey, guys, great performance since the six-minute mark," Coach Blue voiced out in their locker room. "Let's keep this pace going the whole second half, guys. Okay, it's time to head back out on the court to start the third quarter."

Both teams were back on the court, warming up for the second half.

"Girls, this game is a close one," Good Pass voiced out to the rest of the girls.

"I know, girl," Set Shot responded.

"Yes, we agree, child," Block and Dunk voiced out.

The game horn sounded off; both teams rushed to the benches for instructions from their coaches.

"Okay, guys, let's continue to do good out there and stay focused," Coach Blue declared to his starters.

"Okay, Coach," his starters responded.

Both teams returned to the court to play. Texas Tech had the basketball, setting up a low screen play near their basket, and made two points. The score was now forty to forty-two; Texas Tech cut the lead within two points. The whole third quarter was no more than a two-point game.

"Time out! Time out!" Coach Blue shouted out to the official.

Both teams returned to their benches with one minute and ten seconds left in the third quarter.

"Hey, guys, we're slacking up a little on defense," Coach Blue voiced out to his starters. "We have the basketball after this timeout. Let's work up one shot and kill some time off the clock. Set up a high screen on the left side for Ice Cream. Cream, drive to the basket and draw a foul as well."

"Okay, Coach," Ice Cream responded.

The game horn sounded off; both teams were back on the court. USC had the ball, Fats running the point. USC were passing the ball around to one another, killing time off the clock. There were now thirty-five seconds on the clock in the third quarter. Range approached at the high screen on the left side. Range set the screen for Ice Cream, and he received the pass from Fats. Ice Cream was driving the ball toward their basket and made the bank shot off the glass with the foul.

"Yes! Yes, Ice Cream! Great play!" Coach Blue shouted from the bench.

"Yes, honey, yes!" Good Pass was juiced up at her seat.

Ice Cream approached the free throw line to shoot and made both free throws with no problem.

"Yes, baby, yes!" Good Pass responded after his two swish free throws.

Ice Cream put his team up four points with twenty-eight seconds left. Texas Tech had the ball, rushing back down their end to score, but did not score in time. The game horn sounded off at the end of the third quarter; both teams returned to their benches.

"Great play, guys. We have our lead back up." Coach Blue was steamed up. "We have a four-point lead. Let's continue to focus on our shots."

The game horn sounded off to begin the last and final quarter; both teams returned to the court. USC had the ball. During the first seven minutes, the game was very close; with one minute and forty-five seconds left, USC was still leading, sixty to fifty-eight. USC put on a great performance on defense. Texas Tech had the ball, rushing down their end, and made two points to tie the score.

"Time out!" Coach Blue shouted out to the official. "Hey, guys, we slipped again and let Texas tie this game. My goodness!" He was astonished at his team. "Okay, fellas, let's do this. Cream, you keep the ball. We have one minute and nine seconds left in this game. Everybody else, take your man all the way on the weak side. Range, as soon as Ice Cream passes the free throw line, you come over for a give-and-go play. Cream will pass you the ball to score, Range."

"Okay, Coach," Range responded.

The game horn sounded off; both teams were back on the court with under a minute left. Ice Cream received the ball from Deep out of bounds. Ice Cream dribbled to the other side of the free throw line; his teammates recognized the start, moving on to the other side of the court. With twenty-nine seconds remaining, Range began to come over to start the give-and-go play.

"Okay, fellas! Go now!" Coach Blue shouted out to Ice Cream and Range.

Ice Cream passed the free throw line, and Range set the pick-to-pass to him. Range took off to the basket to shoot, and he was fouled but missed his shot on the way up. He had a one-and-one with fifteen seconds left on the game clock.

"Okay, Range, make this free throw shot!" Coach Blue was fired up.

"Okay, Range, baby, make this!" Dunk shouted from her seat.

"You can do it, Range!" Ice Cream and Fats voiced out to him at the free throw line.

"Yeah, man, knock this down!" Deep and Marvin also voiced out to Range.

Range approached the free throw line and took one bounce and made it.

"Yes, sir, Range!" Coach Blue and the teammates shouted from the bench.

"Yes, Range, my sweetheart!" Dunk shouted as well from her seat.

Everybody was jumping up and down, cheering at Range's one free throw shot. He took his second free throw shot and swished it with no problem.

"Yes! Yes!" Coach Blue was overjoyed.

The score was now sixty-two to sixty, USC back up two points with still fifteen seconds to go. Texas Tech rushed hard up their end of the court but missed a wild shot. Marvin grabbed the rebound, and the game horn sounded off to end the game. Everybody rushed to the court to celebrate the victory.

The rest of the season, USC had a great year, advancing to the final four championship game against the powerful Duke Blue Devils.

"Okay, guys, here we go again at the final four championship game, reaching our goal." Coach Blue was excited for his team.

"Yes, sir, Coach. It's amazing, what is happening," Ice Cream responded in the locker room.

"Okay, fellas, there are a lot of people out there. The noise is crazy. Let's keep it tight and shoot well," Coach Blue supervised to his guys. "Let's get out there and win!" He was steamed up.

"Yes, sir, Coach!" the team responded.

The dream boys and their teammates were more than ready to win another title.

"Hey, man, let's win this game and play hard!" Fats shouted out to his teammates in their huddle.

"Okay, fellas, it's time to head out there to warm up," Coach Blue directed.

Both teams exited their locker rooms to the court to start their free throw warmups.

"Oh man, it is packed in here," Deep voiced out softly to Ice Cream.

"Hey, man, I see, but stay focused," Ice Cream voiced out to Deep.

The game horn sounded off; both teams rushed to the benches for instructions from their coaches.

"Okay, fellas, we are here again. Let's do this and beat this Duke team," Coach Blue declared.

"Yes, sir, Coach!" the whole team responded.

The game horn sounded off; both teams returned to the court at the jump circle to start. USC won the toss and made two points right away from Ice Cream's ten-foot jump shot. Duke rushed down their end and made two points as well. The whole first quarter was a close game, like the Texas Tech game earlier during the regular season. Duke was up by four points; the score was thirty-two to twenty-eight by the end of the first quarter.

"Okay, guys, we are in the game. Just play harder and continue to shoot well," Coach Blue stated. "Keep making our free throws. That's what's keeping us in this game so far, guys."

The game horn sounded off; both teams were back on the court. USC had the basketball.

"Pass the ball quickly, guys!" Coach Blue shouted out to his team.

Fats received the ball from Range, coming off the high post screen, driving hard to the basket. He was fouled by Duke with seven minutes and twenty seconds left in the second quarter.

"Take your time, Fats!" Block clamored from her seat.

Fats approached the free throw line and received the ball from the official. He made both free throws like butter.

"Yes, Fats!" Coach Blue screamed.

"Yes, baby, yes!" Block shouted out to him from her seat.

The score was now thirty to thirty-two; USC was down two points. The Duke team were bringing the ball up the court on their end, rotating the ball to one another.

"Okay, guys, great passing!" Duke's head coach voiced out to his team.

Duke took a ten-foot corner shot but missed it badly. USC grabbed the rebound by Range, pushing the outlet to Deep. Ice Cream was running wide, left side, on the fast break play; he received the ball and began driving toward the basket and was fouled with five minutes and thirteen seconds left before halftime.

"Okay, Cream, baby! You know what to do!" Good Pass shouted out from her seat while Ice Cream approached the line.

He made both free throws—all swish with no problem.

"Yes, baby, yes! That's my man!" Good Pass screamed, jumping and cheering.

"Yes, sir, Cream!" Coach Blue shouted along with the teammates from the bench.

The score was now a tie, thirty-two to thirty-two. Duke was coming down their end with the ball, stalling for a couple of seconds, studying USC's defense.

"Watch the pick!" Coach Blue shouted out.

Duke reversed the pick play and passed the ball, weak side, to their shooting guard and made two points. Duke was leading by two points with three minutes and twenty-five seconds before halftime.

USC was coming down their end, taking their time, setting up the offense play. Time was running out, with two minutes and thirty-five seconds left. Deep had the ball, coming off the pick from Ice Cream. He was making eye contact with Ice Cream, but Duke broke the pick. Deep still had the ball, driving to the basket, and was fouled by Duke. Deep approached the free throw line, looking very focused. Duke was up thirty-four to thirty-two with one minute and forty-eight seconds left.

"Okay, Deep. Make these free throws," Ice Cream whispered to him with a high five.

"Okay, Deep, baby! Do it again!" Set Shot shouted out.

He made both free throws with no problem.

"Yes, Deep!" Coach Blue and the teammates voiced out from the bench.

"Yes, baby! Good free throws!" Set Shot was overjoyed in her seat.

It was a tied game, thirty-four to thirty-four. Duke had the ball coming down their end, stalling the ball again, with forty seconds left before the half.

"Okay, guys, start your offense!" Duke's coach shouted out to his team.

USC's Range fouled Duke's point guard to stop the clock with twenty-five seconds left. Duke's point guard approached the free throw line and missed both shots. USC grabbed the rebound, coming down their end now. Fats had the ball, approaching the left side of the court. He passed the ball to Range, who was cutting across the center free throw lane. He received the pass and threw a head fake all at once. Duke's player blocked Range's shot but could not control his balance, coming down, landing on Range and fouling him.

"Good fake, Range!" Coach Blue voiced out to him.

"Okay, Range, make these two free throws!" Block shouted out from her seat.

Range approached the free throw line and made both free throws easily.

"Yes, sir, Range!" Coach Blue was fired up.

"Yes, baby!" Block was overjoyed along with the rest of the girls.

USC gained the lead, thirty-six to thirty-four; with less than ten seconds left, Duke could not score at the buzzer. USC was leading at halftime; the dream boys were trying to win their second final four title.

"Great comeback, guys!" Coach Blue was juiced up in their locker room. "Hey, listen up. Let's try to keep up this lead and upset Duke winning this championship. Okay, guys, huddle up, and let's head back onto the court."

USC's basketball team and Duke's basketball team arrived on the court, warming up their free throws for the third quarter. The game horn sounded off; both teams rushed to their benches.

"Okay, fellas, let's do this and win two titles," Coach Blue instructed his team in the huddle.

The game horn sounded off; both teams were back on the court to start the third quarter. Duke's team had the basketball, passing it around to one another, looking for a good shot. They spotted out their power forward down low, and he made two points. Duke tied the game, thirty-six to thirty-six. USC was coming up their end and made two points as well. USC was back in the lead, thirty-eight to thirty-six; the dream boys' free throw percentage combined was 100 percent.

The rest of the third quarter was very close, with one minute and fifteen seconds left, USC still leading, sixty-eight to sixty-six. Duke had the ball, passing it around, trying not to cause a turnover. Duke made two points to tie this championship game, sixty-eight to sixty-eight, with thirty-five seconds left in the third quarter. USC was coming, pushing the ball up fast toward their end. Deep had the ball, driving quickly to the basket. He lost the ball off his right leg, going out of bounds. Duke had the ball, pushing it up hard with fifteen seconds left, and made a fifteen-foot jump shot at the buzzer. Both teams rushed back to their benches, getting ready for the final quarter of this championship game.

"Listen up, guys. I was getting nervous at one point." Coach Blue was feeling agitated. "Okay, let's continue to shoot well and play good defense."

"Okay, Coach," his starters responded.

The game horn sounded off; both teams were back on the court to start the fourth quarter. USC had the basketball, setting up their offense for a good shot. Ice Cream received the pass from Fats, and he made two points.

"Great shot, Ice Cream!" Coach Blue walked back and forth from the bench sideline.

USC now led seventy to sixty-eight, hopefully to get a comfortable lead later in this game.

"Coach, this is a high scoring game," the bench players voiced out to him.

"I know, guys. We are shooting the ball well against Duke," he responded.

Duke had the ball down their end of the court and made a twenty-foot jump shot. The score was a tie again, seventy to seventy. Duke was not letting up to lose this championship game. With five minutes and thirty-five seconds left to play, the score had increased to eighty-seven to eighty-six, down to the one-minute mark, with Duke leading now, hopefully to win this title. Both teams were making basket after basket 90 percent of the whole fourth quarter.

"Time out!" Coach Blue shouted out to the official.

Both teams returned to their benches for instructions from their coaches.

"We now have one minute and ten seconds left to win this game, guys," he declared. "Let's set up a high pick for Ice Cream to get fouled."

"Okay, Coach," his starters responded.

"Ice Cream, make this one-and-one free throw, son," Coach Blue voiced out to him.

"Okay, Coach. I will make it," Ice Cream indicated, looking serious.

The game horn sounded off; both teams were back on the court. Everybody in the arena was standing up, on their feet, cheering for their team to see who would win this championship game. USC had the ball. Fats was taking his time controlling the offense. He glanced at the game clock and then noticed Coach Blue's signal to start the play. With thirty-five seconds left, Fats waved to Range to set the high pick for Ice Cream. Fats passed the ball to Ice Cream, and he moved off the pick. Ice Cream tossed the ball over to Range, and he under-passed the ball back to Ice Cream. Ice Cream received the ball and went up for a five-foot bank shot and missed but was fouled by Duke.

"No way!" Duke's coach shouted, and he slammed his towel on the sideline.

"Okay, Cream and Range! Great pick play!" Coach Blue was steamed up with joy.

With ten seconds left, Ice Cream approached the free throw line to shoot one and one. All the women, parents, and girls were covering their faces with their hands.

"Okay, honey, you can do it." Good Pass dropped her hands for a second.

"Take your time, Ice Cream," Coach Blue voiced out softly from the bench.

Ice Cream squared up at the line, took one bounce, and swished it through the net.

"Oh my goodness!" Good Pass cheered loudly along with the girls and parents and all the USC fans.

"Yes, sir, Cream!" Coach Blue shouted with the bench teammates.

The score was now eighty-seven to eighty-seven; he had one more free throw shot. Duke fans were making loud noises to get Ice Cream nervous and make him lose focus. Ice Cream squared up again to shoot his second free throw shot.

"Good follow-through, Cream!" Coach Blue noticed his shot after the release from his hands.

He swished it again through the net with no problem. All the USC fans were cheering very loudly with his teammates and Coach Blue.

"Get back! Get back!" Coach Blue shouted.

Duke got the ball back, rushed up the court to their end, and took a wild twenty-footer and missed at the front of the rim. The game horn sounded off, and the game was over. USC won another final four title for the second year. Everybody for USC rushed down to the court, hugging one another, celebrating. Ice Cream was made MVP of the game, and the parents and girlfriends were crying their hearts out. The dream boys had done it again in their sophomore year. The sports reporters were interviewing the dream boys and Coach Blue. After everything began to clear away, Coach Blue's USC team headed to their locker room.

"Guys, we've done it again!" Coach Blue shouted out loud with a high voice. "Great free throws, Ice Cream."

"Thank you, Coach Blue," Ice Cream responded.

"Listen up, guys. Great season. Plus, you all did great tonight," Coach Blue announced to his team.

"Thank you, Coach," the whole team responded.

"Let's pack up and get out of here to celebrate this second final four," Coach Blue stated. "Also, let's get it again next year. We are making history right now, guys." Coach Blue was steamed up.

"Yes, sir, Coach!" The team was juiced up and overjoyed.

After everyone left the arena, they went out to celebrate their victory.

The rest of the school year went great for the dream boys and the girls. The fantastic four continued to work on their free throws after the season. When September came around, Coach Blue called a meeting to plan for the third year. The dream boys and their girlfriends were going into their junior year at USC. When November came around, it was time for basketball to start again. Coach Blue called his first practice, getting ready for the first game against Oregon State University.

"Hey, guys, welcome back again. Great season last year!" Coach Blue declared. "Let's work hard today and be ready for Oregon State on Saturday."

Coach Blue's team had a good practice; plus, their shots and free throws were looking good this season.

"Okay, guys, we have our first game here on Saturday. Let's report here at noon. We have to go to their arena," he stated.

"Okay, Coach," the team responded.

When Saturday arrived, Coach Blue's team arrive on time to leave for Oregon State University. They arrived there, heading to their locker room, getting dressed for the game at 4:00 p.m.

"Okay, guys, we are here. Let's pray," Coach Blue voiced out.

After the prayer, Coach Blue gave his instructions for the game plan. "Okay, guys, huddle up!" He was steamed up. "Okay, listen up. Let's get out here and show Oregon we are champs."

"Yes, sir, Coach," the team responded.

Both teams arrived at the court to warm up their free throws. The game horn sounded off; both teams rushed to their benches.

"Okay, guys, my starters, let's win!" Coach Blue was steamed up.

The game horn sounded off again; both teams arrived back on the court at the jump circle. USC won the toss, setting up their offense, passing the basketball around to one another, looking for a good shot.

"Great shot, Fats!" Coach Blue voiced out.

Oregon State were coming down their end of the court to set up their offense and made two points as well. By the end of the first quarter, Oregon State was leading by eight points. Both teams were at their benches, getting instructions from their coaches.

"Okay, fellas, we are down by eight points," Coach Blue stated. "We have to improve our defense and make good shots. Keep making good free throws. That's important."

The game horn sounded off to start the second quarter. Oregon State had the ball, leading twenty-eight to twenty. Oregon State were running their offense very well, and they made two points again. USC were pushing the ball up their end, trying to come back, and cut this ten-point lead before halftime.

"No, Range, No!" Coach Blue was agitated at him. "Bad shot, son!" He was very shocked.

Oregon State rebounded the ball, pushing it back down their end, and made two points again. The score was now thirty-two to twenty; Oregon State was up twelve points, with four minutes and thirty-two seconds left before halftime. USC were coming back down their end with the ball to make something happen.

"Time out! Time out!" Coach Blue shouted out to the official. "What happened, guys?" Coach Blue was looking soberly at his team. "We did not accomplish anything these last six minutes!" he screamed out loud. "Come on, guys. Let's get back into this game, man!"

The dream boys were looking very silent along with their teammates, wondering what to accomplish out there. The game horn sounded off; both teams were back on the court with two minutes and twenty-five seconds left before halftime. USC had the basketball, setting up their offense, working the ball around. Ice Cream received the pass from Deep and made a fifteen-foot jump shot.

"Great shot, Cream! Let's go, dream boys!" Coach Blue shouted out from the bench.

USC cut the lead to ten points, with Oregon State coming down their end, trying to score again. They missed the ten-foot jump shot. USC grabbed the rebound, pushing it back down their end. Fats had the ball, driving hard to the basket, creating his shot, and made it with the foul from Oregon State.

"Yes, sir, Fats!" Coach Blue's spirit was built up.

USC now cut the lead down to eight points, thirty-two to twenty-four.

"Fats, baby! Come on, guys! Let's get back!" Block shouted from her seat.

Fats approached the free throw line and made his free throw, which cut the lead to seven.

"Yes, Fats! Good free throw!" his teammates shouted from the bench.

With one minute and twelve seconds left before halftime, Oregon State received the ball back, pushing down their end. They missed again. USC were now playing good defense for these last few minutes. USC grabbed the rebound, pushing it hard up their end, running their offense.

"Okay, guys! Let's move the ball!" Coach Blue voiced out to his players.

Deep received the pass from Ice Cream, driving hard to the basket, and was fouled by Oregon State.

"Okay, Deep! Good move!" Coach Blue voiced out.

Deep approached the free throw line to shoot two free throws.

"Okay, Deep, baby! Make these two free throws, honey!" Set Shot shouted out from her seat.

Deep made both free throws with no problem.

"Yes! Yes, Deep!" Set Shot voiced out loud.

"Yes, sir, son! Good free throws! We need them!" Coach Blue shouted.

USC were coming back in the game, only down five points with fifty-eight seconds left. The score was now thirty-two to twenty-seven, Oregon State still holding this lead. Oregon State had the ball, passing around to one another to get a good shot.

"Okay, men, take your time!" Oregon State's head coach voiced out.

All at once, Ice Cream still had the ball, pushing it down their end for a layup. He made the layup and was fouled by Oregon State.

"Yes, baby! Right on!" Good Pass shouted out.

"Yes, Cream, Yes!" Coach Blue was fired up from the bench.

The USC fans were waking up, cheering, back in this game. Ice Cream approached the free throw line with twenty-five seconds left before halftime. He swished both free throw shots like butter. USC was now down two points, thirty-two to thirty.

THE ICE CREAM SHOOTER STORY

"Yes, honey! Good free throws!" Good Pass voiced out.

Oregon State were pushing the basketball up their end to score, but they made a turnover out of bounds. USC received the ball back, pushing it up their end with thirteen seconds left. Ice Cream received the pass in the corner from Fats, and he made it at the buzzer.

"Yes, Cream, Yes!" Coach Blue and their teammates shouted out as they rushed back to their locker room.

"Yes, Cream, baby!" Good Pass shouted out, and the other girls were cheering as well.

USC made a marvelous comeback to tie this game at halftime, thirty-two to thirty-two.

"Great! Great! Great comeback, fellas!" Coach Blue was overjoyed, and the team were jumping around in their locker room. "Okay, fellas, listen up," Coach Blue verbalized to his team. "Let's go out here in the third and fourth quarters and win this game."

"Yes, sir, Coach!" the whole team responded.

Both teams arrived back on the court to start the third quarter. Oregon State had the basketball down their end, setting up their offense, and made two points. USC had the ball coming back down their end, Fats controlling the offense, looking for a cutter. Ice Cream noticed an open area near the free throw line and cut to it. Fats noticed Ice Cream cutting and passed the ball to him. Ice Cream received the pass and faked his shot and was fouled by Oregon State.

"Okay, Cream!" Good Pass shouted from her seat.

Ice Cream approached the free throw line and swished both free throws in with no problem.

"Yes, sir, Cream! Great free throws!" Coach Blue voiced out.

The score was still a tie, thirty-four to thirty-four. The whole third quarter was very close, but toward the end, USC pulled in front by two points, finishing the third quarter. The dream boys were doing very well at the free throw line. While both teams were at their benches, getting ready for the fourth quarter, the cheerleaders were doing their cheers for their team.

The game horn sounded off; both teams were back on the court to start the last quarter. Oregon State had the basketball, setting up their offense, and made two points. Oregon State tied the game with seven minutes and thirty-five seconds left. Both teams were making baskets back and forth as well as making their free throws. USC

had the ball, coming up their end, Fats handling the ball. Deep was
setting up a screen for Ice Cream. He came off the screen, but the ball
was stripped from behind. Oregon State stole the ball, pushing it up
their end, and made two points. Oregon State led the game fifty-six
to fifty-four with six minutes left to play. USC came back down their
end of the court. Range received the pass from Fats. He shot and
missed, but Deep grabbed the offense rebound, put it back up, and
made two points with a foul from Oregon State.

"Yes, Deep, son!" Coach Blue shouted out from the team bench.

"Yes, Deep, baby, yes! Make these free throws!" Set Shot was fired
up with the girls.

Deep approached the free throw line and made his one free
throw shot.

"Yes, baby!" Set Shot cheered.

The score was now fifty-eight to fifty-seven, USC leading by one
point. The game was close all the way, but Oregon State regained
the lead by four points, sixty-two to fifty-eight, with one minute and
fifteen seconds left.

"Time out! Time out!" Coach Blue shouted out to the official.
"Hey, guys, we are down four points. Let's get a steal and score—then
one stop."

Both teams were back on the court; USC had the ball. Fats was
controlling the offense; USC were passing the ball around for a good
shot. Ice Cream received the pass from Range in the corner; he made
a ten-foot jump shot.

"Yes, Cream, yes!" Coach Blue was elated. "Okay, guys, let's get
this ball back!" he shouted out with thirty-five seconds left.

The score was now sixty-two to sixty; Oregon State still had the
lead. USC were playing pressure defense and stole the ball from
Oregon State, rushing it up the court with twenty seconds left.

"Time out! Time out!" Coach Blue voiced out.

The USC fans were cheering very loudly for their team.

"Okay, guys, let's set up a low screen play for Range to score
and make the free throw shot," he declared. "Range, son, use the
backboard when you shoot your shot."

"Okay, Coach. Will do," Range responded.

The game horn sounded off; both teams were back on the court.
The Oregon State fans were cheering out loud for their team as well.

Ice Cream took the ball out of bounds and threw it to Fats. Ice Cream ran down low to set the screen for Range. He came off the screen, receiving the pass from Fats.

"Okay now!" Coach Blue shouted out.

With eight seconds left, Range made the bank shot and was fouled by Oregon State.

"Yes, Range, yes!" Coach Blue was steamed up.

"Yes, Range, baby!" Dunk shouted out from her seat.

Everybody for USC was cheering very loudly, hugging one another. The game was a tie, sixty-two to sixty-two, Range approaching the free throw line. Everybody was standing up, cheering for their team. Range took one bounce and let it go—all swish through the net.

"Yes! Yes! Yes!" Coach Blue shouted.

"Yes, Range! Yes, that's my man!" Dunk shouted out from her seat, jumping up and down along with the other girls.

USC was up one point with eight seconds left. Oregon State were pushing the ball up the court, trying to score but with no hope, throwing a wild shot from twenty feet. The game horn sounded off; everybody for USC rushed to the court, cheering and hugging one another, celebrating the victory. The USC team grabbed Range and picked him up, raising him high above the crowd, rejoicing. Coach Blue and his wife and all the parents were jumping for joy as well. After the celebration eased down, Coach Blue directed his team to the locker room.

"Wow, fellas! This was a great game. Range, you got us out the hole, man!" Coach Blue was fired up.

"Thank you, Coach," Range responded.

Coach Blue and his USC team pack up and left to go back home.

The rest of the season went great for them, and they advanced to the final four again for the third year in a row. The final four tournament came around, and USC made it to the championship final against Michigan State.

"Okay, guys, here we are again for the third year," Coach Blue voiced out to his team in their locker room. "Let's get out here and win another final four, fellas!"

"Yes, Coach Blue, yes!" the whole team responded.

Both teams arrived at the court to warm up their free throws. Michigan State were determined to break USC's final four winning streak. The game horn sounded off; both teams rushed to their benches.

"Okay, fellas, let's keep focus like we've done the last two years," Coach Blue verbalized. "Keep making our free throws. Our percentage is still making history around the world."

The game horn sounded off; both teams arrived back on the court at the jump circle. Michigan State won the toss, pushing the ball down their end, and quickly made two points. USC had the ball coming back up their end; Fats made two points for USC. Michigan State had the ball again, running their offense, and they made two points again. USC were coming down their end with the basketball, Fats handling the ball at the point. He looked left at Ice Cream, passing the ball to him. Ice Cream quickly drove past the defender and was fouled.

"Okay, Cream! Let's make these free throws!" Coach Blue voiced out.

Ice Cream approached the free throw line, squared up, and swished both free throw shots in.

"Yes, Cream, my man! Yes!" Good Pass shouted out from her seat.

"Okay, Cream! Good free throws!" Coach Blue and the team shouted out.

The score was a tie so far at the start of this game, with seven minutes and ten seconds left in the first quarter. Both teams were playing very aggressively to win this championship game. The whole first quarter was close now; with one minute and twenty-five seconds left, Michigan State led by four points, twenty-six to twenty-two. USC had the ball. Range was setting a high screen for Deep to receive the pass from Ice Cream. Deep received the pass and began to drive toward the basket. He pulled up the five-foot jump shot and was fouled.

"Okay, Deep, my sweet man!" Set Shot shouted out.

"Okay, Deep, let's do it!" Coach Blue voiced out.

Deep approached the free throw line and swished both free throws. The score was now twenty-six to twenty-four; USC was down two points with twenty-five seconds left in the first quarter. Michigan State had the ball, pushing it fast up their end to score before the first quarter end. Time ran out; Michigan State did not get a good shot. USC had been playing great defense since the game began.

Both teams were arriving at their benches, getting instructions from their coaches.

"Okay, fellas, we are down two points. Let's continue to play good defense," Coach Blue verbalized to his team.

The game horn sounded off; both teams were back on the court to start the second quarter. USC had the ball, passing it around to one another looking for a good shot.

"Watch him! Watch him!" Coach Blue shouted out from his bench.

Michigan State were cheating over to stop Range from driving. Range reversed his dribble and cut around the double team. He flashed quickly to the sideline, approaching the basket, and was fouled.

"Okay, Range! Good move!" Coach Blue vocalized.

"Okay, Range, baby! Let's get it!" Dunk shouted out loud from her seat.

Range approached the free throw line and swished both free throws.

"Yes, son!" Coach Blue cheered.

The whole second quarter, USC did not let Michigan State get too far. With forty-five seconds left before halftime, Michigan State was still leading by six points, fifty to forty-four. USC had the basketball, pushing it up their end. Ice Cream had the ball. He passed it to Fats and began to cut down the middle free throw lane. Fats passed it back to Ice Cream; he made a ten-foot jump shot with twenty-five seconds left.

"Good shot, Ice Cream!" Coach Blue voiced out.

"Nice shot, Cream, honey!" Good Pass shouted out.

The score was now fifty to forty-six, Michigan State still holding on to that lead. Michigan State were pushing the ball back down their end and made two points at the buzzer. Michigan State were running off the court to their locker room, happy as larks. USC were walking slowly to their locker room.

"Look, fellas, we are still in this game." Coach Blue relaxed his tone. "We are down six points. Keep your heads up, guys. Let's get out there and continue to play good, okay?"

"Yes, sir, Coach," the whole team slowly responded.

Both teams were arriving back on the court to start the third quarter. USC had the basketball, passing it around to one another. Fats spotted out Deep getting open. He fake-passed to Deep and began to drive hard to the basket. Fats was fouled by the Michigan State point guard.

"Okay, Fats! We need these free throws, buddy!" Coach Blue voiced out.

Fats approached the free throw line and swished both free throws.

"Okay, Fats! That's what I am talking about!" Coach Blue shouted.

"Okay, Fats, my sweetie! Great free throws!" Block was fired up at her seat with the girls.

The score was now fifty-two to forty-eight with six minutes and thirty-five seconds left to play. The rest of the third quarter, Michigan State was still leading as they were going into the fourth quarter. Both teams were at their benches, getting instructions from their coaches for the start of the fourth quarter. The game horn sounded off; both teams were back on the court. Michigan State had the basketball coming down their end. They set up a double screen play and scored two points. The front end of the fourth quarter, Michigan State was still holding on to a great lead. Now with three minutes and fifteen seconds left to play, USC were looking a little shaky out there, wondering about whether they would be losing this championship game.

"Time out!" Coach Blue shouted to the official. "Listen up, guys. Let's get back in this game and win," he stated to his starters. "We can do it, fellas. Trust me."

The game horn sounded off; both teams were back on the court. USC had the ball, Fats controlling the offense. He passed it to Ice Cream, and he began driving hard to the basket and was fouled. Michigan State was still up six points, fifty-four to forty-eight, looking for a championship title.

"Okay, Cream, we need these free throws bad!" Coach Blue voiced out to him.

"Come on, man! Please make these free throws!" one benched team member voiced out.

Ice Cream approached the free throw line, took one bounce, and swished both free throws.

"Yes! Yes!" Coach Blue cheered.

"Yes, baby, yes!" Good Pass shouted out from her seat.

The score was now fifty to fifty-four, USC down by four. Michigan State had the basketball with two minutes and ten seconds left in this championship title. USC came up with a steal and pushed the ball up to Range. He knocked down a ten-foot jump shot.

"Yes, Range, yes!" Coach Blue was steamed up.

"Yes, Range! I love it!" Dunk shouted from her seat, the girls cheering.

The USC fans were on their feet, cheering very loudly. The score was now fifty-four to fifty-two, USC closing in with under two minutes to play. With one minute and twenty-five seconds left, Michigan State was trying to kill time with the basketball. They caused an easy turnover to give USC a closer chance to come back. Coach Blue called a timeout.

"Okay, fellas, we are back in this game like I mentioned at halftime." Coach Blue was fired up. "We have one minute and twenty seconds left. Let's score here and get a steal off the double team."

"Okay, Coach Blue!" the starters responded with joy in their eyes.

The game horn sounded off; both teams were back on the court. USC had the basketball. Ice Cream came off the screen play and made a twenty-foot jump shot.

"Yes, sir, son!" Coach Blue shouted.

"Yes, baby, yes!" Good Pass also shouted from her seat.

All the USC fans were standing up, cheering, "Defense!" to Michigan State's offense.

The score was now a tie, fifty-four to fifty-four. The USC team made a great comeback with forty-five seconds left. Michigan State had the ball, killing time to win this championship. USC was playing great defense with twenty seconds left. A Michigan State player took an eight-foot jump shot and missed. Deep grabbed the rebound outlet to Fats. He pushed the ball across half the court with ten seconds left. Fats spotted Deep cutting across the middle free throw lane. Fats passed the ball to Deep. He faked the shot and began to drive toward the basket. He shot and was fouled by Michigan State.

"Yes, Deep, yes! You can do this!" Coach Blue shouted, jumping up and down with the teammates.

"Yes, Deep! Yes, my honey!" Set Shot was also overjoyed, the girls cheering on.

With five seconds left on the clock, Deep approached the free throw line. He took one bounce and made his one-and-one free throw shot.

"Yes, baby, yes!" Set Shot shouted.

"Yes, Deep, son! Yes!" Coach Blue and the team were fired up.

He made his second free throw shot, all swish. The score was now fifty-six to fifty-four; USC had made a wonderful comeback to lead this game. Michigan State pushed the ball up their end of the court and threw a wild shot but no mercy. The game horn sounded off. USC won three final four championship titles. Everyone for USC rushed to the court, crying and cheering and hugging one another. Deep was the MVP of this game. The USC team exited to their locker room after the presentation part.

"Yes! Yes! Yes, we are champs again!" The whole USC team were juiced up in their locker room.

Coach Blue made another great season going into the dream boys' junior year at USC. The rest of the school year went great for the boys and their girlfriends. The dream boys continued working on their free throws going into their senior and last year at USC. It was time for the new basketball season to start. The dream boys felt like they were ready to make history, winning four final four championships.

"Welcome back, fellas. The last three years have been super!" Coach Blue stated. "This is the last year for Ice Cream, Fats, Range, and Deep. Let's win one more for them. Okay, fellas, let's have a good practice today. Our opening game is Stanford University at home."

Later, Coach Blue said, "Okay, guys, practice went very well today. Our free throw percentage is looking great. The game on Saturday is at 3:00 p.m. Let's meet here around 1:00 p.m."

"Okay, Coach!" the whole team responded.

When Saturday arrived, the team was there on time like Coach Blue had mentioned.

"Okay, fellas, Stanford is a good shooting and defensive team," he stated to his players in their locker room. "We have to be the same for them as well."

With one hour and a half gone by, Coach Blue was ready to report to the court. He supervised his team at the bench huddle. "Okay, guys. I love you all, man. Let's go out here and win today!"

Both teams were at their benches, ready for the horn to blow. The game horn sounded off; both teams arrived on the court at the jump circle. USC won the toss, coming up their end, setting up their offense. Range received the pass from Ice Cream and made a ten-foot jump shot.

"Yes, Range! Good shot!" Coach Blue voiced out.

"Yes, Range, my dear!" Dunk shouted out from her seat.

Stanford had the basketball, coming down their end, setting up their offense, and made two points. USC were coming back down their end, looking relaxed.

"Okay, guys, looking good out there!" Coach Blue was watching his team.

Fats was handling the ball and spotted out Ice Cream breaking the strong side under the basket. He passed it to Ice Cream, and he made a twenty-foot jump shot.

"Yes, Cream! Good shot!" Coach Blue and the team shouted out.

"Yes, Cream, honey!" Good Pass voiced out.

Stanford were coming back down their end and made two points again. The game was a tie so far, eighteen to eighteen, with five minutes and twenty-eight seconds to play in the first quarter. USC received the ball back down their end. Ice Cream had the ball, looking for Deep on the block. He bounce-passed it to Deep. He spun around to shoot and was fouled.

"Okay, Deep, baby! Make it happen!" Set Shot shouted.

"Okay, son! Good move!" Coach Blue voiced out.

Deep approached the free throw line and took one bounce and swished both shots.

"Yes, son! Good free throws!" Coach Blue shouted out.

"Yes, Deep, baby, yes!" Set Shot was fired up as well.

USC was up two points with three minutes and eighteen seconds left in the first quarter. Stanford had the basketball. They were passing the basketball quickly to one another making USC work hard on defense. Stanford's point guard pulled up a fifteen-foot jump shot and missed. Range grabbed the rebound with an outlet to Fats, pushing it quickly up the court. USC's new starter, Earl—along with Ice Cream, Fats, Deep, and Range—flashed to the ball side. They set a double screen for Earl to receive the ball from Fats. Fats passed the ball to Earl; he took a ten-foot jump shot and made it. USC was now up twenty-two to eighteen with one minute and forty-five seconds left to play. Stanford had the basketball, running their offense, looking for a good shot. Two Stanford players were setting a high screen near the free throw line. One player was coming off that screen and made two points to bring Stanford within two points. USC were coming back down their end, running their offense with one minute left in the first quarter.

"Okay, guys, keep executing! Stay focused!" Coach Blue vocalized to his starters.

Earl had the ball, looking for Ice Cream coming from the weak side, and he passed the ball to him. Ice Cream received the pass from Earl and began to drive toward the basket. He took a jump shot from the free throw line and made it and was fouled by a Stanford player.

"Yes, sir, Cream! Great shot!" Coach Blue shouted from the bench.

"Yes, Ice Cream, baby!" Good Pass shouted from her seat, the girls cheering too.

Ice Cream approached the free throw line, took one bounce, and swished his one free throw shot.

"Great free throw, Ice Cream!" Coach Blue and the benched team players shouted.

"Yes, baby! Nice shot!" Good Pass voiced out.

The score was now twenty-five to twenty, USC up five points with twenty-five seconds left in the first quarter. Stanford had the basketball, coming back down their end. Their power forward received the pass from his point guard. He took a ten-foot jump shot and missed. The Stanford center player grabbed the offensive rebound to put back, and he also missed at the buzzer. That was the end of the first quarter, USC still holding the lead. Both teams rushed back to their benches for instructions from their coaches.

"Okay, fellas, looking good out there. Stay focused," Coach Blue directed.

The game horn sounded off; both teams were back on the court to start the second quarter. USC had the ball, setting up their offense, Fats handling the ball. He began to drive toward the basket but spotted out Deep in the low post, throwing an underpass to him. Deep received the pass, faked his shot, and began to drive toward the basket to shoot but was fouled by a Stanford player.

"Okay, Deep! Good move!" Coach Blue voiced out to him.

"Yes, Deep, honey!" Set Shot was fired up.

Deep approached the free throw line, took one bounce, and swished his first free throw. He swished his second one just the same.

"Yes, Deep, yes!" Set Shot shouted out from her seat.

"Yes, Deep, son!" Coach Blue blurted out from his bench.

The team's bench players were rejoicing as well. USC was holding a six-point lead with seven minutes and ten seconds left to play before halftime. Stanford had the basketball coming up their end of the court, passing the ball around, looking for a good shot.

"Let's get it, guys!" their head coach shouted from his team bench.

Stanford's point guard split the double team from USC's defense, driving toward the basket, and lost the ball. Ice Cream stole the ball off the turnover from the Stanford point guard. USC were pushing the ball up their end, Deep breaking wide to his right to receive the pass from Range and slam-dunk it in.

"Yes, Deep!" Coach Blue was steamed up.

"Yes, Deep, baby!" Set Shot shouted, jumping up and down from her seat.

The other girls and the parents plus Coach Blue's wife were cheering as well. The score was now twenty-nine to twenty; Deep's two free throws plus the slam dunk had increased USC's lead to nine. With five minutes and twenty seconds left before the half, Stanford was looking a little confused on the offense. They had the basketball, passing it around, focusing on their big guys to score. Stanford's power forward had the ball, looking at his center teammate, posting on the ball side. He passed it to his center, who was six-foot-eight, and he made two points. Stanford cut the lead to seven, twenty-two to twenty-nine. USC came down their end with the basketball, Fats controlling the offense. Deep came up to set a pick for Ice Cream near Fats. Fats saw the pick, and he passed the ball to Ice Cream. He drove hard toward the basket and was fouled by a Stanford player.

"Okay, Cream! Good move!" Coach Blue was steamed up at the bench.

"Okay, baby! Let's get it at the line!" Good Pass was fired up.

Ice Cream approached the free throw line and swished both free throws with no problem. Ice Cream put USC back up nine points, thirty-one to twenty-two, with two minutes left before halftime. Stanford came back down their end with the basketball, looking for their big guy to score again. Stanford's point guard was dribbling toward his big center teammate to give him the basketball. He received the ball, beginning to drive, and was fouled by Range. He approached the free throw line and made one out of two shots. The score was now twenty-three to thirty-one, USC still holding on to the lead with forty-five seconds left before halftime.

USC came down their end, setting up their offense, hoping to score before the half. Down to twenty seconds left, Fats spotted out Ice Cream in the corner. Ice Cream popped out near Fats to receive the pass. He drove toward the basket and drop-passed the ball to Deep. He received the pass, turned around to shoot, and was fouled by a Stanford player.

"Yes, sir, Deep! Good move, son!" Coach Blue blurted out.

"Yes, Deep, yes!" Set Shot shouted from her seat.

With eight seconds left, Deep approached the free throw line. He took one bounce and let it fly. Deep made both free throws, all strings, with no problem.

"Yes, Deep! Great free throws!" Coach Blue was fired up.

"Yes, Deep! I love it!" Set Shot voiced out from her seat.

The score was now thirty-three to twenty-three, Coach Blue's USC team up ten points. Stanford were pushing up their end quickly to score, but time ran out. The game horn sounded off for halftime. Both teams arrived at their locker rooms to plan for the second half.

"Guys, wonderful first half!" Coach Blue was elated with his team. "I like what I am seeing. Let's keep this lead up, fellas."

"Okay, Coach," the whole team responded.

"Okay, guys, let's get back out there for the second half and win!" Coach Blue was fired up.

Both teams were back on the court, warming up for the second half. The game horn sounded off; both teams rushed back to their benches, getting instructions from their coaches.

"Okay, fellas, let's continue this lead and keep shooting good free throws," Coach Blue directed.

The game horn sounded off; both teams were back on the court. USC had the ball. USC were passing the ball around, looking for good shot. Ice Cream had the ball, looking for Range, cutting across the middle free throw lane. Range cut across and received the pass and turned around to shoot and made two points.

"Yes, Range, yes!" Coach blue shouted.

"Yes, baby!" Dunk was steamed up from her seat.

The score was now twenty-three to thirty-five; USC was up a dozen points. Coach Blue was pleased with his team. USC was leading the whole third quarter, going into the fourth quarter, still by a dozen points. Late in the fourth quarter, with two minutes and thirty-five seconds left, Stanford came back to cut USC's lead to two points.

"Time out! Time out!" Coach Blue shouted out to the official. "What is going on out there, fellas?" Coach Blue was looking agitated. "Come on, fellas! Get your heads back, guys!"

The game horn sounded off; both teams were back on the court. USC had the ball.

"Okay, fellas! Work for a good shot!" Coach Blue blurted out from the bench.

Fats was controlling the offense with two minutes and five seconds left. The USC fans were wondering what would happen. Fats passed to Ice Cream; he began to drive toward the basket to shoot, but he under-passed the ball to Deep. He missed the five-footer. Stanford grabbed the rebound, rushing down their end, and made two points. The score was now sixty-eight to sixty-eight, with one minute and ten seconds left to play in the fourth quarter. USC were coming back down their end, setting up their offense. Fats, handling the ball, looked left and passed to Range. Stanford came up with a steal, pushing back up their end, and made two points.

"No! No!" Coach Blue shouted out, stamping his feet.

The score was now seventy to sixty-eight; Stanford had regained the lead. With forty-five seconds left, Coach Blue called a timeout.

"Okay, guys, we have time to score and play good defense," he declared. "Okay, listen up. After we score to tie this game, let's get the ball back to Fats and let him finish up."

The game horn sounded off; both teams were back on the court. Fats was handling the ball at the court, looking for Ice Cream. Ice Cream cut left, Fats pushing his dribble to his left side and chest-passing to Ice Cream. He caught the chest pass and made a twenty-foot jump shot.

"Yes, Cream, yes!" Coach Blue shouted.

"Yes, baby, yes!" Good Pass also shouted out.

The score was a tie. With twenty-five seconds left, Stanford had the ball, holding it for the last shot. USC were playing tight man-to-man defense. Everyone in the arena was standing up, feeling nervous about their team. Stanford's point guard was looking to his right to pass to his teammate. Fats came up with the steal, pushing the ball back down their end to score, but was fouled by Stanford.

"Yes! Yes! Yes! Yes, Fats!" Coach Blue was elated, jumping up and down, along with the team at the bench.

"Yes, Fats, my honey! Yes!" Block shouted from her seat along with the girls.

The score was still a tie in the last twenty-five seconds. Fats approached the free throw line, shooting a one-and-one. He took one bounce and swished his first free throw shot.

"Yes! Yes, Fats! Finish up, son!" Coach Blue shouted from his team bench with the teammates.

"Yes, baby, yes!" Block also shouted, jumping for joy with the girls.

The USC fans were cheering very loudly. Fats began to shoot his second free throw and swished it again.

"Yes, my man, Fats!" Coach Blue was fired up, knowing he had this game.

"Yes, baby, yes! Good free throws!" Block was juiced up.

With three seconds left, Stanford were rushing up the court with the basketball quickly, but the game horn sounded off; time had run out. USC fans rushed to the court along with the girls and the teammates. A couple of men were picking Fats up among the crowd, cheering and celebrating the win.

After everything was over and they all went home, the rest of the season went great for Coach Blue. USC advanced again for the fourth year, heading to the final four championship. This was college basketball history for USC, attending four final four championship-title games. USC advanced to the final championship against Kansas. The dream boys had made history for their college team, USC.

The superdome was packed tonight. Coach Blue's team and Kansas arrived at their locker rooms. All the sports network crews around the country were here to see this historic game.

"Okay, guys, first of all, I have to say I've loved you all for four years," Coach Blue stated. "It has been a great pleasure meeting our dream boys. Ice Cream, Fats, Range, and Deep, you guys have blessed my heart since I met you guys at the ice cream store."

"Thank you, Coach. We love you too!" the dream boys responded.

"Keep shooting those free throws. One day you guys will be professional free throw shooters and trainers," he affirmed to them.

"Thank you, Coach Blue," the fantastic four replied.

"Okay, guys, let's pray," Coach Blue voiced out to his team. "Okay, fellas, let's do this one more time for the fantastic four going out their senior year. On three—four final fours!"

After Coach Blue's speech, they began screaming their way out onto the court to warm up. Also, Kansas were cheering their way out to break USC's winning final four streak. The game horn sounded off; both teams rushed to their benches to get instructions from their coaches.

Coach Blue supervised his starters. "Okay, fellas, this is it. Let's have fun and play!"

The game horn sounded off; both teams arrived back on the court at the jump circle. The fans were clapping and cheering for their teams. USC won the toss, coming down their end, setting up a play. Fats was handling the ball, looking for Ice Cream, cutting around the low screen. He passed to Ice Cream, and he made a ten-foot jump shot. Kansas were coming down their end with the basketball, running their offense. The point guard spotted out the big man down low, and he made two points. USC were back up their end. Range had the ball, driving hard to the basket, and was fouled by Kansas.

"Yes, sir, Range!" Coach Blue shouted out.

"Yes, Range, baby!" Dunk also shouted from her seat.

Range approached the free throw line and took one bounce and swished his first shot. He took his second free throw and swished that one too.

"Yes, Range! Good free throws!" Coach Blue voiced out.

"Yes, Range, yes!" Dunk cheered.

Kansas were pushing the ball up their end and made two points again. The score was a tie, both teams starting out on fire, making basket after basket. USC were coming back down their end, setting up their offense.

"Okay, fellas, watch the double team!" Coach Blue shouted out to his team.

Fats escaped to the other side, looking for Deep to pop up at the high post. Deep received the pass from Fats. He began to drive hard to the basket and was fouled.

"Okay, Deep! Good move, son!" Coach Blue shouted out.

"Yes, Deep, my man!" Set Shot was steamed up along with the girls.

Deep approached the free throw line, took one bounce, and let it fly—all swish, both shots.

"Yes, Deep! Good free throws!" Coach Blue voiced out.

"Yes, Deep, baby, yes!" Set Shot was fired up.

The whole first quarter and second quarter had very close scores, both teams no more than six points apart, USC leading at halftime by four points.

"Okay, guys, great first half. Way to stay focused and take good shots!" Coach Blue stated. "Also, our free throw percentage has been super since day one four years ago. Let's get out there and win this final four championship title!" Coach Blue was steamed up.

"Yes, sir, Coach!" The whole team was fired up and ready.

Both teams were back on the court, warming up for the second half. The game horn sounded off; both teams rushed back to their benches, getting instructions from their coaches.

"Okay, fellas, let's stay focused for one more half and win four history titles!" Coach Blue was fired up.

The game horn sounded off; both teams were back on the court to play. Kansas had the ball, coming down their end, setting up their offense. They made two points, closing the gap to two. USC came back down their end. Fats had the ball and passed to Range. He took a ten-foot jump shot. It bounced off the rim. Kansas grabbed the rebound, pushing it up their end, and made two points. The score was now a tie, thirty-eight to thirty-eight, with five minutes and thirty-five seconds left in the third quarter.

USC were coming back down their end. Ice Cream had the ball and bounce-passed to Deep on the block. He caught it and spun around to shoot but passed it off to Range. He received the pass to shoot, but his shot was blocked by a Kansas player. Kansas stole the ball, rushing back down their end, and made two points. USC came back down their end and lost it out of bounds.

"Come on, guys! Wake up!" Coach Blue shouted from the bench.

The score was now forty to thirty-eight. Kansas took the lead with two minutes and ten seconds left in the third quarter. Kansas had the ball back on their end and made another two points with one minute and forty-five seconds left at the end of the third quarter.

The Kansas fans were cheering very loudly, saying, "We are the champs!"

USC were coming back down their end, setting up a play for Ice Cream to score. Fats was running the offense, looking for him on the left side. Fats lost control of the ball; Kansas stole it and rushed back down their end and made another two points. The score was now forty-four to thirty-eight; the Kansas fans were really going crazy in this arena. With fifty seconds left in the third quarter, Kansas was up six points. USC were coming back down their end to score. Coach Blue was sitting down, looking a little bit nervous, and the team on the bench looked nervous too. The girls suddenly became silent, along with the parents. Range had the ball and spotted out Deep on the low block. He passed the ball to him, and he traveled with it.

"Oh no, fellas, what are you guys doing?" Coach Blue look very dejected because of what his team were doing out there.

Kansas had the ball back down their end with fifteen seconds left and made two points again. The score was now forty-eight to thirty-eight; Kansas had a ten-point lead at the end of the third quarter. Both teams were at their benches, getting ready for the final quarter of this championship game.

"Look, guys, I am very upset by how we gave up ten points." Coach Blue was looking sincere. "We have eight minutes to come back and do something. Let's get out there and make something happen and play defense."

"Okay, Coach," the starters responded.

The game horn sounded off; both teams were back on the court to start the fourth quarter. USC were bringing the basketball up their end, looking to score. Fats was controlling the offense; he spotted out Range, posting up. Range received the pass and started to drive toward the basket but lost the ball. Kansas stole it, throwing a long court pass down their end to their point guard. He laid it up and made two points. Kansas was up a dozen with seven minutes and twenty-five seconds left of winning the title. USC came back down their end. Fats had the basketball, looking for Ice Cream. Ice Cream broke out to the left corner, receiving the pass from Fats. He made a twenty-foot jump shot to bring USC back within ten points.

"Good shot, Cream!" Coach Blue voiced out.

"Yes, Ice Cream, baby! Do not give up, honey!" Good Pass shouted from her seat.

Kansas were coming up their end, setting up their offense. USC were playing tight man-to-man defense, looking very serious now. Kansas's point guard bounce-passed to their power forward, but Ice Cream stole the ball and passed it to Fats. He, at center court, was looking on both sides, spotting out Range to his left. He received the pass from Fats and made a ten-foot jump shot. The score was now forty-eight to forty; USC cut Kansas's lead to eight.

"Okay, guys! You are waking up now!" Coach Blue shouted out from the bench.

"Yes, Range, yes!" Dunk blurted out from her seat.

With five minutes and thirty-five seconds left, Kansas had the ball, looking down low to their big guys. Kansas's six-foot-ten player received the pass from their power forward. He shot, but it hit the front of the rim. Deep grabbed the rebound and passed it to Fats. He was running up their end and spotted out Ice Cream in the corner again. Ice Cream shot another twenty-footer and made it.

"Yes, Cream, yes!" Coach Blue was fired up.

"Yes, Cream, baby!" Good Pass cheered along with the girls.

The score was now forty-eight to forty-two with four minutes and ten seconds left to play. The USC fans were coming back alive, cheering very loudly. Kansas were coming back down their end, setting up a play. Fats and Ice Cream double-teamed the point guard and stole the basketball. With a two-on-one play, Fats went wide, drawing Kansas's defender to him. He passed the ball to Ice Cream at the free throw line. He drove hard to the basket and was fouled by a Kansas player.

"Yes, Cream, son!" Coach Blue shouted out.

"Yes, Cream, baby! We need these free throws!" Good Pass blurted out.

Ice Cream approached the free throw line, took one bounce, and swished his first shot. He did it again, shooting his second free throw shot.

"Yes, sir, man!" Coach Blue was fired up with joy.

"Yes, Cream, honey!" Good Pass was also fired up.

The score was now forty-eight to forty-four; USC had made a big turnaround, down by a dozen earlier. With two minutes and thirty-five seconds left to go, Kansas were coming down their end, feeling defensive pressure from USC. Ice Cream stole the ball again and rushed all the way back down their end for a layup and was fouled.

"Yes, Ice Cream, yes!" Coach Blue cheered.

"Yes, Cream! Yes, baby!" Good Pass also cheered with joy along with the girls.

Ice Cream approached the free throw line, squaring up, took one bounce, and swished his first shot. He reset his second free throw and swished that one as well with no problem. The score was now forty-eight to forty-six, USC within two points. Kansas had the basketball coming down their end, setting up their offense. USC were playing very tight defense, looking for a steal or turnover opportunity to get the ball back.

"Okay, boys! Look for a good shot!" Kansas's coach voiced out.

"Right there, Ice Cream! Get it!" Coach Blue shouted out to him.

Ice Cream cheated over in the passing lane and stole the ball from Kansas's point guard.

"Yes, Cream! Push it!" Coach Blue shouted out.

Fats received the ball from Ice Cream, controlling USC's offense. Ice Cream ran down to the block and V-cut back to Fats. Fats spotted Ice Cream and passed the ball back to him. He shot twenty-five feet out and made it.

"Yes, Cream, yes! Good shot!" Coach Blue was juiced up with joy.

"Yes, baby! All right!" Good Pass was fired up with the girls.

The USC fans were really back in this game with one minute and twelve seconds left in this championship. The score was now forty-eight to forty-eight. Kansas were coming back down their end, moving the ball around, looking for their power forward. He received the pass, driving to the basket, and was fouled by USC. He approached the free throw line, shooting a one-and-one shot. He made his first free throw shot but missed his second one. The score was now forty-nine to forty-eight, Kansas leading with forty-five seconds left. USC were coming back down their end.

"Time out! Time out!" Coach Blue voiced out to the official. "Okay, fellas, we have twenty-five seconds left to win this game. Fats, you handle the point and look for Ice Cream. Look for Cream coming from the weak side."

"Okay, Coach," the starters responded.

The game horn sounded off; both teams were back on the court. USC had the ball with twenty-five seconds left, trying to win four straight final four games. Range was throwing the ball to Fats from out of bounds. Fats reset the offense at the top of the key, looking for Ice Cream. With ten seconds left, Ice Cream flashed from the weak side to the strong side of the ball. Fats threw a chest pass to Ice Cream, Kansas trying to steal it. Ice Cream received the pass and began to drive hard toward the basket. He was fouled by the Kansas power forward before the shot.

"Yes, Cream! Good move!" Coach Blue shouted out.

"Yes, Ice Cream, baby, yes!" Good Pass screamed from her seat with the girls.

With three seconds left, Ice Cream approached the free throw line, looking serious. He squared up his body and took one bounce to make the one-and-one free throw shot. Everyone in the arena was standing up, but the Kansas fans were making all kinds of noise to distract and make him miss that one-and-one free throw. Ice Cream shot his first free throw, all swish.

"Yes, sir, son!" Coach Blue was fired up with joy with the teammates.

"Yes! Yes! Yes!" Good Pass shouted, jumping up and down from her seat with the girls.

The USC fans were cheering all over the arena. Ice Cream received the ball from the official to shoot his second free throw. The score was a tie, forty-nine to forty-nine. Ice Cream could put his team into making history. Ice Cream squared up again and let it fly in the air to the basket. It floated to the basket, all swish. USC took the lead, fifty to forty-nine, with three seconds left.

"Yes, buddy, yes!" Coach Blue shouted from his bench with the teammates and everybody for USC.

"Yes, my man, yes!" Good Pass shouted; she was all over the place, jumping up and down from her seat with the girls.

The USC fans were ready to sprint to the court to celebrate the victory. Kansas had the ball back, pushing up their end fast, and took a wild shot, but there was no hope for them. Time ran out, and the game horn sounded off. USC won the championship title. USC made college history, winning four final four championships.

The USC team rushed to the court, cheering and shouting with all the fans. The girls rushed to their dream boys, hugging them. The parents and Coach Blue's wife were hugging one another. Ice Cream was made MVP and college free throw shooter of the year. After all of the celebration eased down, USC received their fourth final four championship trophy in a row.

Coach Blue's team slowly arrived, shaking hands at their locker room before undressing and closing out the dream boys' college career.

"Hey, guys, this has been a wonderful four years for all of us," Coach Blue declared. "Especially our seniors—Ice Cream, Fats, Range, and Deep. Dream boys, I want to thank you guys from my heart for being here. You fellas are great free throw shooters. Also, you will all be pros one day. Continue to shoot your free throws to get better and better."

"Thank you, Coach, for what you've done for all of us," Ice Cream voiced out to him.

"You are welcome," Coach Blue responded.

The rest of the college school year went beautifully for the dream boys and the girls. As they were approaching the end of their college career, it was time for college graduation day.

Chapter 14

COLLEGE GRADUATION DAY

When graduation day arrived, the parents and family members and friends arrived back in LA. The dream boys and the girls were looking very nice for graduation. They met in the parking lot before graduation began.

"Hey, sons! You guys look handsome," the dream boys' parents declared.

"Our girls look beautiful too," the girls' parents mentioned as well.

The USC arena was packed with people on behalf of USC winning four final four championship titles. The graduation ceremony began. Coach Blue arrived on stage.

"Good evening, everyone," he voiced out to the people. "I am grateful to bring home four final four championship titles. Four of my players have done a great job at the free throw line since they arrived here. Let's congratulate these four guys. Stand up, fellas—Ice Cream, Fats, Range, and Deep."

Everyone began to cheer out, "Free throw shooters! Free throw shooters! Free throw shooters!"

The girls started saying it, and then everyone followed them. It took around two minutes to calm everyone back down in their seats.

"I have known these four men since I met them at the ice cream store when they were young," Coach Blue stated. "These four men will be professional free throw shooters one day."

When graduation day came to a close, the dream boys and the girls received their college degrees. They took their caps off and tossed them in the air.

"Hey, guys, us parents will give you all and the girls too a nice graduation cookout at Ice Cream House," the parents declared to them.

"Oh, wow! That sounds great!" The dream boys and the girls were overjoyed.

They all finished celebrating and left USC to go home for the graduation cookout.

Chapter 15

GRADUATION COOKOUT

After the dream boys and their girlfriends unpacked their college things, the parents began to plan the cookout. The next weekend, on that Saturday afternoon, everybody arrived at Ice Cream House. The dream boys and their fathers put up the tints, tables, and, most surely, the basketball goal. The girlfriends and their mothers prepared the food for the cookout. A lot of friends and some college friends arrived to celebrate the cookout too.

"Hey, guys, will you all shoot free throws at this cookout?" the fathers asked.

"Sure. That's why we want the goal up," the dream boys responded.

"Okay, guys, let's get it up," the fathers replied.

After they finished putting up the basketball goal, Ice Cream rushed inside the house to get his basketball.

"Hey, man, let's do a short free throw workout," he voiced out.

"Okay, Cream. Sounds great," his teammates responded.

The fantastic four began to shoot their free throws, making them one after another.

"Look out there, ladies! Those boys still got it," Block's mother articulated.

The girlfriends noticed as well. "Yes, they can still shoot."

Everyone began to come around the court to watch the dream boys shoot their free throws. Ten minutes before the boys had begun to shoot, the local sports reporters arrived at the cookout. They got word that the final four champs were performing their free throw workout at the cookout. While the dream boys were shooting, the sports crew began taking pictures and video-recording their free throw shots. The music was playing, and everyone began cheering while the boys were shooting their free throws. The dream boys were shooting one hundred free throws apiece at 97 percent. At the same time, people were dancing, eating, and watching the fantastic four shoot those free throws. Later that evening, it was getting dark, and the graduation cookout was coming to a close. All the friends and sports crew began to pack up and leave. The dream boys and the girls were packing up everything to get ready for church on Sunday.

Early on Sunday morning, they all attended Ice Cream's church. The dream boys were walking in with their Bibles in one hand and their basketballs in the other.

"Good morning, men and women," the pastor voiced out to the dream boys and the girlfriends. "We have been tuning in to all of your college games. Congratulations on winning four final four championships!" the pastor cheered.

The church began to say, "USC! USC! USC!" They shouted very loudly, supporting the dream boys.

"Man, this seems like a real game," Ice Cream whispered to his teammates.

After church, they all went back to Ice Cream House. The dream boys and the girls took a ride to the ice cream store for a visit. When they arrived at the store, the customers began to clap and shake the dream boys' hands.

"We saw the game on television. You guys were great!" the customers declared.

"Thank you all for your support," the dream boys responded.

The store manager gave them free cones of ice cream. They sat down to eat their cones. They sat at the same table they had when they were young men and women.

"Hey, everybody, this is nice. This brings back memories." Ice Cream was overjoyed.

"Yes, it does, Cream," the rest of the crew responded.

"Hey, Ice Cream, watch this!" Fats verbalized. He balled up his napkin and shot it into the trash can.

"Oh, wow! How could we not forget that, Fats?" Deep shouted.

The dream boys began to shoot their paper balls into the trash can like back in the day.

"You guys will grow old and still be shooting paper balls," the girlfriends declared.

They had fun at the ice cream store for a while.

"Okay, Manager and everybody else here, have a nice day!" the crew announced.

They left, riding back home, getting ready for summer work.

Chapter 16

THE NATIONAL FREE THROW
SHOOTING TOURNAMENT LEAGUE

After two weeks had gone by, the dream boys and their girlfriends began to work. They were all working at the same company, Nike Basketball. The store manager had been watching the dream boys play college basketball. The store manager gave them new gear from head to toe to wear.

As the years went by, the dream boys and their girlfriends became older in life. Thirty years later, the crew were still working at the Nike Basketball company. The fantastic four never stopped shooting their free throws and continued with their dream of becoming professional free throw shooters one day. Coach Blue and his wife had also gotten older, but they were still in great shape. The dream boys and girls kept themselves up very nicely for all these years. The parents were disabled a little bit, not able to do the things they could years ago.

This weekend, the dream boys and the girls were off work, resting at Ice Cream House, talking about old times, shooting free throws.

"Ice Cream, your phone is ringing, man," Fats voiced out to him.

"Hey, you guys, it's Coach Blue!" Ice Cream was thrilled.

"Hey, Ice Cream, how are you?" Coach Blue voiced out to him on the phone.

"I am fine," Ice Cream answered.

"Listen up. I was selected to coach this new basketball league," he declared.

"Oh, wow, Coach!" Ice Cream was overjoyed.

"Tell the rest of the guys the good news."

"Okay, Coach Blue, right away," he responded. "What is the new basketball league called, Coach?"

"It's called the National Free Throw Shooting Tournament League," Coach Blue voiced out.

"Oh, that's nice! I like that." Ice Cream was steamed up.

"The president of the league told me he needs four free throw shooters to represent the U.S. team," Coach Blue declared. "He wants you guys to be on his U.S. team. You guys will shoot free throws for our country!" He was elated.

"Okay, Coach. We will be glad to shoot," Ice Cream responded.

"I will fly you guys and the girls back here to LA," he affirmed. "Our practice will be at the Los Angeles Staple Center. The president also told me you guys will be contracted for eighty-five million dollars for the whole tournament."

"Oh, wow, Coach! That's amazing. Thank you!" Ice Cream shouted out loud.

"Hey, man, what's wrong with you in there?" Deep blurted out.

"Hey, Coach, I'll talk to you later." Ice Cream was delighted over the news.

"Okay, Cream. Congratulations to you guys!" Coach Blue voiced out to Cream, closing the call.

"Hey, guys, I have wonderful, great news from Coach Blue," Ice Cream affirmed.

"What, Cream?" they all responded.

"Coach Blue will be the head basketball coach of this new league out now," he stated. "It's called the National Free Throw Shooting Tournament League."

"Oh, wow! We are ready, Cream!" Fats cheered.

"The president of the league wants us to shoot for our country," Ice Cream verbalized.

"Wow, man! This is a knockout!" Fats shouted.

"This is wonderful, guys!" the girls also shouted out.

"Also, we will be on an eighty-five-million-dollar contract for this national tournament!" Ice Cream blurted out loud.

"Oh my goodness!" the whole crew shouted.

"Hey, guys, we have to practice our free throws and retire from Nike Basketball." Ice Cream was overjoyed.

"Yes, sir, Cream. Let's do this now!" Range and the rest were steamed up.

The dream boys and the girls would be leaving Friday morning at eleven o'clock. They all retired from Nike Basketball that week, and the boys practiced a lot of free throws. When Friday morning arrived, the dream boys and their girlfriends were waiting at Norfolk Airport. They said their goodbyes to their families and friends back home. When the crew arrived on the plane, everyone began to stare at them.

"Excuse me, sir. I remember you guys shooting free throws," one of the plane staff workers said. "You are Ice Cream, right?"

"Yes, I am," Ice Cream responded.

"How old are you guys now?" the plane worker asked Ice Cream.

"We all are in our fifties now," he responded.

"You guys are great free throw shooters. Are you all still shooting free throws?" the plane worker asked.

"Yes, we are going to LA to shoot for our country in the national free throw tournament," Ice Cream declared.

"Oh, wow! That's real nice," the worker replied.

"Thank you," Ice Cream responded.

The dream boys and the girls were sitting on the plane, relaxing, waiting to land. Six hours later, the plane arrived in LA. Coach Blue and his wife were waiting at the gate for them. When the crew arrived inside the airport, they saw Coach Blue and his wife at the gate. They were all happy to see one another, hugging and shouting.

"Wow, Ice Cream, Fats, Range, and Deep, you guys look great, man!" Coach Blue was overjoyed.

"Thank you, Coach," the dream boys responded.

"You girls look great as well." Coach Blue and his wife were elated.

"Thank you very much," the girls responded.

"You, Coach Blue, and your wife look great yourselves." The crew were amazed, looking at them both.

"Thank you," Coach Blue and his wife responded.

They began to head toward the big bus to leave. While they were all walking outside to the bus, Coach Blue still could not believe this.

"Hey, Cream, you guys, are you still 97 percent from the free throw line?" he asked.

"Sure, Coach. We've never stopped shooting free throws, man," Fats affirmed.

"Great, guys. There are some great free throw shooters from other countries in this national tournament," he declared to his dream boys.

They all arrived on the big bus, riding to the hotel near the Staples Center arena. The dream boys and their girlfriends arrived at the hotel, unpacking their things.

"Hey, guys, let's go downstairs to eat and talk about the national free throw tournament," Coach Blue announced to his team.

"Okay, Coach," they all responded.

They all arrived at the food court to eat and discuss the tournament. After Coach Blue discussed the game rules and regulations to his fantastic four, he planned practice on Monday at 10:00 a.m. at the USC arena.

"Okay, guys, my wife and I have to go to the Staples Center to pick up the tournament bracket sheets," he verbalized.

"Okay, Coach," the crew responded.

"Be ready for practice on Monday. I will be here to pick you guys up at 9:30 a.m."

"Okay, Coach," the crew responded again.

Early on Monday morning, the fantastic four and their girlfriends got up out of their beds to be ready for Coach Blue's arrival.

"Good morning, guys!" Coach Blue and his wife as well as the rebounding staff were walking into the hotel.

"Good morning, everybody!" the crew responded.

"You guys ready for practice?" Coach Blue asked his fantastic four.

"Yes, sir, Coach!" They were steamed up, ready for practice.

They all exited to the big game bus, heading to USC for practice.

"Wow! This brings back memories," Ice Cream voiced out.

"Yes, sir, Cream. It does," Deep responded.

When they all arrived at the parking lot, the fantastic four plus the girls reflected on those winning free throw games.

"Okay, guys, let's head to the locker room to get dressed," Coach Blue directed to his team. "Hey, fellas, here are your uniforms for the national tournament."

"Wow, Coach! These uniforms are nice." The dream boys were fired up.

"Also, these are your practice jerseys," Coach Blue announced.

"Wow, Coach! These practice jerseys are nice too." The fantastic four were overjoyed.

The LA sports news crew arrived at USC to film some coverage on the dream boys. The practice was going very well so far; the boys were shooting their free throws like they had done thirty years ago.

"Good job, guys! Way to shoot your free throws with good rhythm!" Coach Blue was juiced up, looking at his team.

Everyone back in Virginia could tune in to their sports channel to see the fantastic four practice for a short moment. The parents were very happy to see their sons shoot free throws for the United States. Ice Cream's dream when he was a little kid to become a professional free throw shooter along with his three first-grade classmates/friends came true.

The rest of the week at practice went great for the dream boys and Coach Blue. There were sixteen countries in this free throw tournament going for the world title. The first round started next Monday at 1:00 p.m. at the Staples Center. The following Monday came around. Coach Blue arrived at the hotel to pick up the crew at eleven o'clock that morning.

"Okay, guys, it's time. You all ready?" Coach Blue voiced out.

"Yes, sir, Coach!" the fantastic four responded.

They all boarded the big bus, riding to the Staples Center. When they arrived there, it was packed with cars all the way around the building. Coach Blue's U.S. team opened up Game #1 against the Canada team. Coach Blue's U.S. team won by a dozen free throws. The fantastic four shot their free throws like butter. Game #2 was France against Brazil, Game #3 was Argentina against Spain, Game #4 was Lithuania against Australia, Game #5 was Nigeria against Great Britain, Game #6 was Tunisia against China, Game #7 was Japan against India, and Game #8 was Bulgaria against Ghana, and that was the first round of the national free throw shooting tournament. The teams that advanced to the second round were Coach Blue's

U.S. team, France, Spain, Australia, Great Britain, China, Japan, and Ghana.

During the second round opening game, the United States versus France, the fantastic four were shooting their free throws like they were nothing at all. Coach Blue was very happy with how his U.S. dream boys were shooting their free throws in this tournament. Coach Blue's rebound staff were doing great as well, throwing zip chest passes to his shooters at the free throw line. Game #2 was Spain versus Australia, Game #3 was Great Britain versus China, and Game #4 was Japan versus Ghana. There were two more rounds in this tournament before the national championship game. The fantastic four had been shooting at a 99 percent team free throw percentage so far in this tournament. The LA sports news crew began to interview Coach Blue during some timeout periods.

"Hello, Coach Blue. When and where did you meet your four free throw shooters?" the sports crew asked.

"Well, I met Ice Cream, Fats, Range, and Deep around twenty to thirty years ago," Coach Blue responded. "My wife and I were at this ice cream store in Virginia for the weekend, visiting family members. I saw Ice Cream and his boys shooting paper balls in the trash can, and they made them ten times in a row. I was excited to see that from such young boys. I have watched these little kids growing up, shooting free throws at 96 percent from the free throw line. That's why today they are pros, shooting for our country."

"This has been a great career for Ice Cream, Fats, Range, and Deep," the sports media crew responded. "These four men can really shoot free throws. It's amazing! We will be tuning in throughout this national free throw tournament."

"Okay. Thank you, guys," Coach Blue responded.

On Thursday night, it was time for the third round with eight teams left. Game #1 was the United States versus France, Game #2 was Spain versus Australia, Game #3 was Great Britain versus China, and Game #4 was Japan versus Ghana. Coach Blue's U.S. team had been shooting very well from the free throw line during this whole tournament. They defeated France by twelve free throws shots. Also, Spain knocked out Australia in their game, China knocked out Great Britain in their game, and Japan knocked out Ghana in their game.

On Friday night, there were four teams left before the championship game—the United States versus Spain and China versus Japan. The dream boys were making their way to a national title, shooting for their country. During the fourth round, the United States knocked out Spain by twenty free throw shots. China knocked out Japan by twenty-five free throw shots. The girls began to cry as they were so happy; plus, all of their family and friends back home were celebrating the U.S. team's victory to the finals. The fantastic four were reaching their dream goal that they had had in life since they were kids in the first grade. The sports media back home in Virginia were advertising this tournament all over the state.

Coach Blue mentioned to his guys while they were watching China knocking out Japan that China were a great free throw shooting team at 98 percent. Coach Blue's U.S. team would be shooting against China for the national free throw world title on Saturday night at eight o'clock. All of the family and friends plus Mrs. Hoops and her family arrived in LA that Friday night at the hotel. They were all ready to see the United States versus China during the Saturday night showdown. After Coach Blue's U.S. team finished watching the China game, they headed back to the hotel to rest for the Saturday night game.

"Okay, guys, it's late, and your families and friends are here at the hotel to see you guys play tomorrow night," Coach Blue declared. "Tell your family and friends I will pick everyone up tomorrow evening at six o'clock to ride on the big bus."

"Okay, Coach Blue. We will," the fantastic four and the girls responded.

Early Saturday morning at the hotel, they all ate their breakfast while getting ready for the game. When 5:50 p.m. came around, they all met downstairs in the main lobby, waiting for Coach Blue.

"Good evening, everyone." Coach Blue and his wife plus the rebounding staff and the cheerleaders arrived at the lobby right at 6:00 p.m.

"Good evening, Coach Blue and everybody else," the fantastic four and everybody with them responded.

"You guys ready to win tonight?" Coach Blue was fired up.

"Yes, sir, Coach! This is what we have been waiting for," the fantastic four answered.

They all exited onto the big bus, riding to the Staples Center, wondering who would win this championship game.

"Okay, fellas, listen up. When we get there, let's hurry into the locker room."

When they all arrived at the Staples Center, Coach Blue and his U.S. team rushed to their locker room to relax for a minute. Everyone else on the bus exited to the court inside the center to have a seat. While Coach Blue and his fantastic four were resting in the locker room, there was a very silent moment.

"Hey, guys, let's win this for God, who got us here, and our families, our friends, our girlfriends, Mrs. Hoops, Coach Blue, and our country!" Ice Cream was steamed up.

After he said his speech, they all began to cheer and clap, ready to shoot.

"Let us pray," Coach Blue voiced out to his team.

After the prayer, it was time for the fantastic four to get dressed and play. The China team were getting ready to come out onto the court as well. Both teams were leaving their locker rooms to warm up their free throw shots on the court. The fans for both teams were packed all around inside the Staples Center. The U.S. fans were cheering very loudly, and the China fans were doing the same while the teams were still warming up.

"Hey, look, girls—our men are looking good warming up!" Block voiced out, fired up.

"Yes, they are. Their shots are looking good too," Set Shot put into words.

"Their follow-through's looking good too," Good Pass declared.

"Also, they are looking serious," Dunk mentioned.

The girls noticed all of the fantastic four's free throw dynamics. The game horn sounded off; both teams rushed to their benches, getting instructions from their coaches. The order of shooting for Coach Blue's U.S. team was as follows. The first quarter shooter was Deep. The second quarter shooter was Range, and the third quarter shooter was Fats. The fourth quarter shooter was Ice Cream.

"Okay, fellas, this is it. Let's win this national title!" Coach Blue delivered to his team in the huddle. "Deep, you will start us off at the free throw line. Keep your focus up, son."

"Okay, Coach," Deep responded.

The game horn sounded off. Deep went out to his free throw line along with two of Coach Blue's rebounding staff members. China's shooter went out to their free throw line with their two rebounders. Two officials arrived, one at each free throw line, down both ends, officiating the game. The game horn sounded off; both shooters began to shoot for ten minutes.

"Hey, man, those four China shooters look like the same shooters that we lost to at the court near the ice cream store," Ice Cream noticed, talking to Fats and Range on the bench.

"Oh, wow, Cream—you are right!" Fats and Deep responded.

"Let's get them back this time," Ice Cream indicated to his teammates.

"For sure, Cream," the teammates affirmed.

"You guys know those China shooters?" Coach Blue asked.

"Yes, Coach. They beat us shooting free throws when we were twelve at the outside court near the ice cream store," Ice Cream voiced out to his coach.

"Okay, let's get them good!" Coach Blue was fired up.

"Hey, look, girls. Those four China shooters are the same guys who beat our men at the outside court back in the day," Good Pass voiced out to the girls.

"For sure they are, girl," Block, Dunk, and Set Shot responded.

Deep and the China shooter were shooting very well with eight minutes left in the first quarter. The score was forty to forty. Coach Blue was watching Deep's free throw dynamics.

"Good shooting!" Coach Blue voiced out.

At the five-minute mark, Deep began to pull away in the lead for Team USA. The United States had a ten-point lead, fifty to forty. The U.S. fans were cheering all over the arena. With under twenty minutes left, Deep made twenty free throws in a row, which increased the lead to seventy to fifty-three. China's shooter made thirteen free throws in a row during that time frame, but it was not enough for him to stay with Deep. Time went by, with thirty-five seconds left in the first quarter. Deep made eight more free throws, but China's shooter missed a lot. The game horn sounded off to end the first quarter. The United States had a good lead, seventy-eight to sixty-three. Both shooters went back to their benches. Set Shot was cheering and shouting along with everybody else for the U.S. team.

"Great job, Deep, shooting your free throws!" Coach Blue voiced out to him. "Way to stay focused with great body balance with your follow-through!"

"Thank you, Coach," Deep responded.

"Okay, guys, we have a fifteen-point lead. Let's keep this up." Coach Blue was juiced up with a happy look on his face. "Okay, Range, you are up to shoot. Let's continue this good free throw shooting."

"Okay, Coach," Range responded.

The game horn sounded off. Range and the second shooter for China arrived at their free throw lines along with their rebounders. The game horn sounded off. They begin to shoot their free throws. Range was on fire while shooting his free throws, but China's shooter was a little slow, starting out by missing some shots. At the six-minute mark, the U.S. team was leading, 103 to 73. Range was continuing that large lead that Deep had left behind in the first quarter. Everyone for Team USA was going crazy, cheering loudly all over the Staples Center. Coach Blue and the team at the bench were getting their hopes up to win this national title.

"Good free throw shooting, baby!" Dunk shouted out from her seat.

The girls were celebrating early, shouting, "USA! National champs!"

China's fans were looking very lost and sad so far in this final game. With ten seconds left before halftime, Range had made twenty-five free throws in a row; China's shooter did the same. The game horn sounded off, and the halftime score was 123 (the United States) to 93 (China). Both teams rushed back to their locker rooms, getting ready for the second half.

"Great job, Deep and Range! Way to stay focused, man!" Coach Blue shouted out. "Okay, Fats, you will open the third quarter, and, Ice Cream, you will finish up the fourth. Okay, guys. One more half. Let's continue to stay focused and bring home this national free throw title."

"Yes, sir, Coach!" the professional free throw shooters responded.

Both teams were back on the court, warming up their free throws to start the third quarter. The game horn sounded off; both teams rushed back to their benches.

"Hey, look, men, I've never seen guys shoot so many free throws in a row like that before," China's coach voiced out to his team about Coach Blue's fantastic four on the U.S. team. "Let's try to come back at some point in this third quarter, guys."

"Okay, Fats, let's get it, man. Go out there and put it in," Coach Blue declared to him.

"Okay, Coach. Will do," Fats answered.

The game horn sounded off; both shooters arrived at their free throw lines with their rebounders. The game horn sounded off for both shooters to start shooting their free throws. Fats started out good, but China's free throw shooter was smoking shots in, one after another. China was coming back, and their fans were waking up, cheering and shouting.

"China is back! China is back!" The China fans repeated that cheer for the last seven minutes in the third quarter.

Fats began to lose his focus, and China was getting closer and closer.

"Fats, come on, man!" Ice Cream shouted out.

"Fats, pick up your rhythm, son!" Coach Blue blurted out as well.

"Oh man, Fats is not focused on his follow-through," Block voiced out to the girls.

"I see, Block." The girls noticed as well.

The score was now 140 to 131, the United States still holding on but only up nine points. With three minutes left, China advanced to take the lead, 158 to 148. Time went down to one minute left. Coach Blue called a timeout.

"Hey, Fats, you feel okay?" Coach Blue asked.

"I feel a little sick, Coach," Fats answered.

"Can you finish up this last minute?" Coach Blue asked.

"Yes, Coach. I will try."

"Okay. Finish up, son," Coach Blue responded.

The game horn sounded off. Fats and the third China shooter arrived at their free throw lines. The game horn sounded off to start. Fats was very slow in shooting his free throws, but the China shooter was still making his shots, one after another. Time ran out to end the third quarter; China had a great lead over the United States. The score was now 178 to 153; Fats had just made five free throws in that last minute. China's shooter had put on a show this whole third quarter; they were up fifteen points. When Fats arrived at his team bench, he quickly received medical attention.

"Okay, Ice Cream. We are down fifteen points. You have to bring us back," Coach Blue declared to him.

"Okay, Coach Blue. I will do my best," Ice Cream responded.

The game horn sounded off; the last two shooters arrived at their free throw lines to start. Fans began to stand and cheer for their teams at this last quarter for the national title. Ice Cream was looking very serious, as was the fourth China shooter. Good Pass was looking kind of nervous along with the girls. The U.S. fans were stunned, wondering what would happen in this last quarter. Ice Cream was looking up at the scoreboard, planning to bring his team back.

"I got your back, Fats." He looked at Fats while standing at the free throw line.

"Okay, Cream! Get it done, man!" Fats voiced out to him.

Then Ice Cream looked up at Good Pass, and she blew a kiss to him. That meant, "Bring the victory home, my man."

Everybody was standing up for the whole fourth quarter, looking at both shooters. Ice Cream began shooting amazingly at the free throw line. China's shooter could not keep up with Ice Cream. The United States began to come back quickly because of Ice Cream's free throw shooting dynamics. The score was now 185 to 178; the United States had cut that lead down to seven points. With six minutes left to play, Coach Blue called a timeout. The U.S. fans were jumping up and down, clapping and shouting, looking happy again.

"Great! Great! Great free throw shooting, Ice Cream!" Coach Blue was juiced up.

"Yes, sir, Cream!" His teammates gathered around him during the timeout period.

"Thank you all," Ice Cream responded.

The game horn sounded off; both shooters went back to their free throw lines.

"Go, Cream, baby, go!" Good Pass shouted from her seat.

All the Virginia fans back home were rejoicing at this game, supporting their U.S. dream boys' team. The game horn sounded off for the shooters to start again. Ice Cream was knocking down free throws like butter, bringing his U.S. team very close to a tied score. Coach Blue was jumping up for joy, along with the girls, their parents, and their friends plus Mrs. Hoops and her family. The score had been 185 to 178, but now it was 190 to 185; Ice Cream had cut the lead to five points with two minutes left for the world title. China's free throw shooter began to lose his focus on his shots.

Ice Cream was still shooting great, cutting China's lead to two points with fifty-nine seconds left in this national free throw world-title game. Good Pass was covering her face, she could not take it. The score was a tie with now twenty-nine seconds left, 193 to 193. Everybody had been standing, on their feet since the quarter began. All the sports reporters in the world were tuning in to this national-title game. Ice Cream and the China shooter were now picking up more of their rhythm; with five seconds left, the score was still a tie, 205 to 205. At the buzzer, China's free throw shooter missed as the ball hit the back of the rim. Ice Cream made his last free throw shot at the sound of the horn, and the game was over.

Everyone for the U.S. team was rushing to the court, cheering and shouting, "USA! USA! USA!"

The girls were hugging their fantastic four boyfriends, celebrating the victory. Coach Blue and his wife were celebrating along with the parents and family members plus friends. The U.S. team received their trophies, and Ice Cream was the MVP of the game. Plus, everyone back home in Virginia was celebrating.

After everyone became silent, Coach Blue made his speech center court. The final score was 206 to 205. The U.S. team won the national free throw shooting tournament league. The final free throw stats were as follows: the United States, 98 percent; Russia, 75 percent; France, 70 percent; Brazil, 80 percent; Argentina, 81 percent; Spain, 88 percent; Lithuania, 74 percent; Australia, 79 percent; Nigeria, 73 percent; Great Britain, 89 percent; Tunisia, 77 percent; China, 93 percent; Bulgaria, 86 percent; Ghana, 84 percent; Japan, 87 percent; and Canada, 78 percent.

Chapter 17

MEET THE NEXT GENERATION

After Coach Blue and his world-title champs arrived back at their locker room, they packed up and met their families and friends in the hallway. When they approached their families and friends, everyone began to cheer for their U.S. team.

"Everyone out here, listen up!" Coach Blue voiced out. "I have really enjoyed coaching these four professional free throw shooters. I've never seen free throw shooters that can shoot like these four guys here in my life. I have won four final four championships and now the national world free throw shooting title. My wife and I have been blessed since we met Ice Cream, Fats, Range, and Deep at the ice cream store in Virginia."

"Coach, we thank you for all you have done for our families and friends," Ice Cream voiced out.

"Thank you, guys," Coach Blue responded.

Everybody began to clap for Coach Blue and his guys for being together for the last time. After everybody finished hugging and crying, they all exited to the big bus. While riding back to the hotel, the national free throw shooting champs were holding up their trophy.

When they arrived at the hotel, everyone else there began to shout, "Champs! Champs! Champs!"

"Okay, guys, it is now finished. You all, flights are ready in the morning at eleven o'clock," Coach Blue stated.

"Okay, Coach," they all responded.

"Hey, guys, you all will teach the next generation's little boys how to shoot free throws," Coach Blue declared.

"Yes, sir, Coach. Hopefully, when we go back home, we will meet some little boys like us," Ice Cream voiced out.

"That will be nice, man!" Fats, Range, and Deep were fired up.

"My wife and I will be back here tomorrow morning to take everyone back to the airport," Coach Blue stated.

"Okay, Coach. Thank you," they all responded.

They began hugging one another and departed.

On that Sunday morning, Coach Blue and his wife arrived at the hotel to take them to the airport. They said their goodbyes, and the fantastic four, the girls, and their families plus friends departed from Coach Blue and his wife. The free throw pros and the rest landed in Norfolk, Virginia, at around 7:00 p.m. They departed from one another and went to their homes.

The national free throw champs and their girlfriends had been friends for a long time since they were kids. One year later, they became husbands and wives. Ice Cream was Good Pass's husband, Fats was Block's husband, Range was Dunk's husband, and Deep was Set Shot's husband. During their honeymoons, they went back to LA to visit Coach Blue and his wife. They also visited the rebounders, the cheerleaders, and their college friends.

"Hey, guys, let's visit the ice cream store on our way back home," Good Pass voiced out.

"Okay, sounds great," the rest of the crew responded.

When they arrived, almost home from LA, they took a drive to the ice cream store. They walked inside to sit down to eat ice cream cones.

Ice Cream noticed something. "Hey, guys, look over there where we sat back in the day. There're four young boys and four young girls," he mentioned. "The young boys are throwing paper napkins in the trash can."

"Yeah, man, just like we'd done thirty years ago," Deep voiced out.

"Yeah, man. Let's go over there," Ice Cream vocalized.

The pros went over to the young boys' table to ask them a question.

"Good evening, young men. We saw you guys shooting your paper napkins into the trash can!" Ice Cream put into words. "Can you young fellas shoot ten times in a row?"

"Sure, we can," one young boy responded.

"What is your name, son?" Range asked.

"They call me Hot Shot," the young boy answered to Range. "This is Goal, this is Buckets, and this is Swish. These are my friends. These girls are our school friends. My girl is Cake."

"My girl is Sweet," Goal voiced out.

"My girl is Cute," Buckets voiced out.

"And my girl is Strawberry," Swish voiced out as well.

"Sir, we have been friends since the first grade," Hot Shot voiced out to the fantastic four free throw world champs.

By that time, Good Pass, Block, Dunk, and Set Shot joined them all at the table.

"Hey Hot Shot, Goal, Buckets, and Swish, you young fellas have nice shots," Ice Cream declared to the young fellows. "You four young fellas will be the next top free throw shooters to represent the United States one day."

"Yes, that's right. We can see it in you boys," Fats, Range, and Deep also declared.

"Thank you all, sir," Hot Shot and his school friends responded.

"We have to go back to the court and practice our free throw shots," Hot Shot voiced out to the pros.

"You young boys do that," Ice Cream declared.

The young boys and their young girlfriends rushed out the ice cream store, heading to the court. Ice Cream, Fats, Range, Deep, and their wives went out behind them in their cars to see the little stars shoot their free throws. The pros and their wives remained in the cars, watching, talking to one another on their cell phones.

"You know what, y'all? Those little stars will be the next 'hot shot shooter story,'" Ice Cream voiced out on the phone to the crew.

"You are right, Cream," the rest of the crew responded on their cell phones.

Ice Cream and Good Pass, Fats and Block, Range and Dunk, and Deep and Set Shot slowly drove away in their cars.

The End of

The Ice Cream Shooter Story

Frank "Hot Shot" Rodgers (the author) started writing this story on February 12, 2012, and ended on January 21, 2015.

About The Author

Frank "Hot Shot" Rodgers was born in Norfolk, Virginia. He grew up in the Bowling Park neighborhood in Norfolk, where he started his education at Bowling Park Elementary School. At a young age, he started playing the sport of basketball with some of his school friends on the playground after school. Frank completed his education in 1983.

As Frank became older, he continued to play basketball and trained basketball players on their free throw shooting skills. As of today, Frank is a free throw shooter coach and an author writing his first book, entitled *The Ice Cream Shooter*. Frank is playing the lead character, Ice Cream, in the story.

Frank has attended many fundraising events, shooting free throws to help raise funds for different organizations. Frank has also attended the National Free Throw Subway Commonwealth Games Contest, and he won the silver metal. Frank is also a multitalented musician. He's been playing various instruments—such as the bass guitar, the lead guitar, the drums, and the accordion—for thirty-five years. Frank was taught to play each of these instruments as well as how to play basketball by his father, Frank Rodgers Sr., and his mother, Doris Rodgers. Although Frank has had many accomplishments as well as some obstacles, he has never stopped loving the game of basketball.

About The Book

The story deals with a seven-year-old kid, Ice Cream, who has marvelous talent. He fantasizes about becoming a professional basketball free throw shooter when he becomes older in life. When young Ice Cream attends first-grade elementary school, he cannot stay focused on his schoolwork because his mind is always on shooting free throws all the time. While in class, he decides to use some of his clean notebook paper and balls it up into paper balls, and he starts shooting them into the trash can near his desk.

While class is going on, three of his classmates—Fats, Range, and Deep—who are sitting near him see Ice Cream shooting the paper balls, and they are very amazed by how young Ice Cream is making those shots in the trash can. Fats, Range, and Deep decide to follow Ice Cream and do the same thing—shooting paper balls in the same trash can. They are all shooting together in class, trying not to let their teacher, Mrs. Hoops, catch them shooting the paper balls. At the same time, there are four girls in the class—Good Pass, Block, Dunk, and Set Shot—who see Ice Cream, Fats, Range, and Deep, and the four girls love the way the boys are shooting the paper balls, making shot after shot in the trash can.

As the years go by, all eight of them become close friends, and the four girls follow Ice Cream, Fats, Range, and Deep all the time, through good times and bad times, going to practices, shooting at events, and going to local basketball courts. They all attend the same high school and college together. When Ice Cream, Fats, Range, and Deep become older adults, their dream of becoming the top four professional free throw shooters to represent the U.S. Olympic Free Throw Shooting Tournament team comes true, and they advance to the national championship-title free throw shooting game to represent their country.

Photo Caption

Frank Rodgers Sr. (The Ice Cream Shooter Father)
He was a professional musician who played the bass guitar with his professional rock band, called the Carolinas, during the year 1961. He was also a furniture refinisher and repair. They called him "the Doc" on his job at the Grand Furniture Warehouse. Last but not least, he taught the game of basketball—how to shoot the ball in the basketball goal he mounted on the pine tree in the backyard in the year 1972.

Doris Rodgers (The Ice Cream Shooter Mother)
She was also a musician, playing the guitar and the button accordion, like her father, Albert Long, and her mother, Fannie Long, natives of North Carolina. My mother also loved basketball.

Shirley Langley (The Ice Cream Shooter Oldest Sister)
She was a professional bowler, and she loved the game of basketball as well. She gave me permission to train her two sons—Marvin and the drum artist, Dion Langley—how to play basketball. Today Dion Langley's son Eman Langley is a great basketball player and a drummer like his father, Dion.

My father and mother and eldest sister passed away before my book was completed.

Made in the USA
Middletown, DE
24 November 2024